Manacle

Chris Aslan has spent many years living in Central Asia. Chris wrote a part memoir part travelogue, called *A Carpet Ride to Khiva: Seven years on the Silk Road*, about life in Uzbekistan and is currently lecturing on textiles, tour-guiding around Central Asia and studying in Oxford for Anglican ordination. Chris's website is www.chrisaslan.info.

Manacle

Chris Aslan

LION FICTION

Published by Lion Fiction
an imprint of
Lion Hudson Ltd
Wilkinson House, Jordan Hill Road
Oxford OX2 8DR, England
www.lionhudson.com/fiction

ISBN 978 1 78264 255 8
e-ISBN 978 1 78264 256 5

First edition 2017

A catalogue record for this book is available from the British Library

Printed and bound in the UK, October 2017, LH26

To Tim Campion-Smith and George Watkinson.
Thanks for everything you've taught me about
running the race.

BEFORE

Chapter One

Light pools in the east behind the silhouetted hills and a breeze comes off the Great Lake rustling the leaves of the vine and pomegranate tree down in your courtyard. You sleep. It's peaceful. But a storm is coming and you don't realize. We know, because we can rise up on thermals and sense changes in the air that you have no idea about. There are lots of things that we know that you don't. Even if you were awake, you wouldn't realize that we're watching you right now. We've passed through the inner room where your mother sleeps, her head covered with a headscarf in the hope it will protect her from evil spirits. What makes her think a headscarf would impede us? We've slipped through walls and passed through the ceiling and now we hover over the flat roof of the house where you and your brother Timaeus are sleeping. Your situation might not be great, but we still watch you with envy. You have something we desperately want: a home.

You wake unbidden and silently shake Timaeus, who takes a little longer to rouse and dress himself. While he pulls on his tunic, you pile up the sleeping mats and bedding.

"Come on," you whisper, climbing onto the low wall that surrounds the roof. You crane your neck towards the water. "The boats are starting to return."

You both run down the stone steps to the courtyard, each grabbing a flat basket and long cloth strip. Slipping into your sandals, you head downwards through the narrow cobbled streets towards the lake path.

"I'll race you," you say to Timaeus, adding, "Here, give me your basket." Even though you both know who will win, it doesn't stop Timaeus from grinning, dropping his basket and bolting away. He runs down the stone steps flanked by boulders, scrub and the occasional stunted olive tree. Then, when the path flattens at the base of the hill, he sprints. Clouds of dust puff up wherever his feet land. He lets the long strip of cloth stream behind him like a banner and you do the same, still clutching the baskets in your other hand as you feel the power in your body and gradually narrow the distance between you and him. It's a joyful scene and it bores us. We follow you anyway, skimming lazily overhead because we too have come for the fish.

We swoop down to the nearing boat, and we feed on the panic and the pain emanating from the piles of fish gasping in the air. It's not much of a meal but it will have to do. One of us dips beneath the waves and sees several large bream lurking under the inviting shadow of the hull. For sport, we give one of the struggling sardines the strength to flip itself overboard. It swims frantically downwards and doesn't even notice the mouth of the bigger fish until it is too late. Snuffed-out hope has always tasted good, even if it's just a fish. But really, we're hungry for more.

As the boat nears the shore, Rufus at the prow gives the call. The men have already removed their tunics and now they tug off their waist cloths before jumping naked overboard, hauling the boat through the waves. You and Timaeus leave bundles of clothing pooled beside your sandals as you run to join them,

Chris Aslan

splashing through the waves. You're taller and move to the stern, putting your shoulder to it. You're determined to play your part, knowing you've just had a good night's sleep while the fishermen are exhausted and chilled to the bone. You catch a glimpse inside the boat where bream and redbellies still flop amid the nets. It's not these larger fish that interest you, but the glistening, seething mass of sardines beneath them. It's been a particularly good catch and you grin as you push the stern hard. You feel sand grinding beneath its keel and grunt with the others as you push the boat forward until it is beached.

"Looks like you'll be making two trips, maybe three," says Rufus, the head fisherman, with a tired smile, cricking his neck and rubbing a knotted muscle in his shoulders.

You grin again and then remember not to invite bad luck. "You've had better catches," you say loudly to the winds in a way he won't find offensive, because he knows you're just wanting to protect yourself from the Evil Eye. The fishermen put their tunics back on and start disentangling the nets, laying them out to dry. Later, Rufus will store them away in a large wooden hut used by all the boats and the only building on the bay. Other boys will come for the bigger fish, but for now you and Timaeus are able to scoop up handfuls of sardines unhindered, depositing them into the centre of each flat basket until the silver mounds threaten to cascade over the sides. You replace your waist cloths – it wouldn't do to walk back to the village naked – but you leave your tunics behind, not wanting them to smell any stronger of fish than they already do.

"Phin, can you help me?" says Timaeus, and kneels before you as you wind the strip of cloth around the crown of his head and balance the basket on top of it. He wrinkles his nose. The smell is overpowering. You return to the village slowly, keeping your backs and necks straight, trying to ignore the fishy water seeping through the basket weave and turban as it dribbles down your wiry back.

If you were aware of us, you'd probably be wondering why we've taken such interest in you. After all, you seem content – almost happy – at least today. But, like we said, we know things that you don't. Some of us have flown higher and we've seen something you don't know about, and we're not just referring to the coming storm. There's a different kind of storm approaching you. It makes your momentary happiness bearable because, like the bream lurking in the shadows waiting for that sardine, we know that a feast is coming our way. You see, we've seen who's making his way back to the village.

"There's still at least four more baskets'-worth down there," says Timaeus, depositing his load onto a worn cloth that your mother has laid out in the courtyard underneath the vine. His hair is wet and smells of fish. He grabs a ladle from the water jar and gulps its contents down. The sun has crested the hills and already the day is warm.

"Have some dates, both of you," says your mother. "We'll eat properly once we've finished salting the fish. Here." Your mother hands you a pouch of coins. "Tell Rufus I've made offerings to the goddess for his catch, and don't buy from anyone else. Oh, and ask him for a basket of redbellies. Look at the sun. Today is a good day for drying them."

She's wrong, of course.

You pass most of the fishermen as you head back down to the lake and they nod to you wearily, ready to sleep. There are other youths with baskets of bream and redbellies on their heads. You notice that Timaeus is tired.

"Let's have a quick break," you say, once you're down at the bay again. Then adding, so he won't think you're doing this for him, "I want to see if I can get that cat to come out."

You wander over to an area of thick undergrowth with a couple of sardines in hand, calling gently. There's no sign of her, so you lay the sardines down and back away. A few moments later the skinny feral cat appears, glances at you warily, and then

Chris Aslan

bolts down the sardines, barely chewing. Her belly is swollen with a litter she'll bear soon. You'd love to take one of her kittens and look after it, but your mother would never allow cats in the courtyard – not with the bad luck they might bring – and anyway, *he* would torment it. He'd probably kill it just to spite you.

"Come on, Phin," Timaeus calls, and you collect another full basket. Despite the weight and the smell, you're grateful for your flat basket, as it shades you from the glare of the sun.

By the time you've returned for the third time, both of you are wet with sweat and fish water. Rufus nods his head towards the lake. "Go on, get yourselves cleaned up. I'll pile the last baskets for you."

Neither of you needs a second invitation and you plunge into the water, splashing each other, tugging off your waist cloths and using them to rub the smell of fish from your bodies as best you can. You emerge dripping but revived, your tight curly hair hanging with the weight of water in it.

"Come here, Phineas," Rufus beckons, as you wring out your waist cloth and tie it back on. You can tell from his tone that he has something he wants to say, and Timaeus shoots you a look.

"Thank you for your help, Uncle," you say politely. "And thanks for putting aside a basket of redbellies for us. We're most grateful."

Rufus waves these pleasantries aside. "It's been a good night for everyone. You could buy as many redbellies as you want from any of the other boats."

"We prefer to purchase the best," you say, and Rufus rolls his eyes at this flattery, although he's clearly pleased. He comes and stands in front of you, a little too close. He's a big man, all beard and corded muscle. "You've still got a little way to go," he says, measuring your height against his. He steps away, his eyes lingering on your fading bruises. Somehow you know from his expression that he's figured out where you got them. "How old are you now, Phineas?"

"Sixteen," you reply, suddenly feeling shy at the way he appraises you. He feels the muscles in your arms, and grunts.

"You've got some filling out to do. Still, I've watched you hauling the boat in each morning and you seem keen." The rest of the conversation seems to be happening inside his head, and it's only when he notices your perplexed expression that he continues out loud. "My older brother says he's getting stiff and sore and wants to move into fish-drying. It's more sociable hours. I'll be a man down."

He turns and lifts up the last basket of sardines while you wait for him to say more. "Well, don't leave me holding this forever." He growls and you hurry to bow before him as he lowers the basket onto your head.

"Uncle Rufus," you say respectfully, "why are you telling me this?"

"Why do you think?" says Rufus gruffly. "You're fatherless and I could do with a strong pair of hands I can trust. It's time you took care of your family. The gods know, someone has to. Talk to your mother and let me know tomorrow." You stand there beaming and it makes Rufus uncomfortable. "Well, off you go then." He shoos you both away.

Timaeus picks up the basket of redbellies and you wait until you're both out of earshot before you let out a little whoop of delight. "I probably should have just said 'yes', right there, in case he changes his mind, but it'll still be good to let Mother know," you say, and Timaeus nods and tries to smile. "What?" you ask. "Come on, Tim, this is such great news."

"I know," he says, his voice trembling. He's on the verge of tears.

"Listen, you'll be able to join me soon. You're tall for fourteen and you're already catching me up."

"Yeah, but you always get there first."

You walk together in silence. "Did you hear what he said about me being fatherless?" Timaeus says nothing. "It means he understands our situation. He's a good man." What Rufus means is that he doesn't buy the pretence of *that man* being your father, or even stepfather. You pause but Timaeus is still quiet. "Please, Tim, can you just be happy for me? I'm finally going to get out."

"I know," says Timaeus quietly, "but I'm not. I'm stuck behind, with *him*."

You suddenly understand why he's so upset. "Listen, I'll still be at home during the day."

"Yes, but at night?"

"I won't let him touch you," you say.

"What are you going to do? You won't even be here," says Timaeus, tears spilling over. You've always managed to place your sleeping mat between Timaeus and him, and fought off at least some of the nocturnal advances he's made towards both of you. We know. We've drunk it up, delighted.

"We'll figure something out," you say. "Look, if I've got a proper job, I'll be bringing in a steady income. I'll ask Rufus to look after my wages. I won't let *him* get his hands on anything. Maybe we can find a way of getting rid of him completely."

"Maybe," says Timaeus. He sighs and then his face takes on that dead-eyed, expressionless look you see so often on your mother when *he's* around.

You get back home with the last of the baskets. "I know you're hungry," says your mother, bending down to lift your basket, "but let's get these salted now. Another hour in this heat and they'll all have turned."

You glance at your mother. She's a short, taut woman, her face already lined by hardship. You're about to tell her your news, but then sense that she'll receive it better once the work is done.

"Right," she says with a sigh, gently pushing the small of her back. "Phin, you gut, I'll salt, and Tim, you can look after the redbellies."

You squat beside the pile of sardines, knife in hand, deftly slitting each belly, thumbing the entrails into a wooden bucket and then passing each sardine to your mother. She rubs sea salt into them, splays them open to dry better and winds them by their tails onto a string. Timaeus does the same thing with the larger redbellies, and soon he's hanging lines of fish up and down the whitewashed walls of your small courtyard, making it look almost festive. The sardines will take two days to dry, the redbellies a little longer.

You work together in companionable silence. All of you are relaxed in a way you can never be when *he's* around. Once the last sardine is hung, your mother cleans her hands and says, "I'll make a start on breakfast. Phin, you take the bucket of offal to Antigona."

You lift the bucket carefully, not wanting to spill any of its evil-smelling contents, and cross the street to your neighbours, eager for an excuse to see Berenice.

"Well, don't look too crestfallen," says Antigona smiling sardonically as you knock and enter their courtyard. She knows you were hoping her daughter would answer. "Don't worry, Berenice is just feeding the piglets. You can join her, if you like."

You brighten, and carry the bucket around the corner towards the sound of squeals and grunts. Most of the herd have been taken foraging by her brother, Justus, but the youngest piglets are kept behind, out of harm's way. Berenice is throwing them food scraps.

She turns and smiles, and you feel funny in your stomach. "I'm trying to be as fair as possible," she says, turning back to the piglets, "and not just let the biggest or the greediest get everything."

"Well, I've got some more food for them."

"Mmm, lovely," she says, wrinkling her nose, but smiling still. "I think we'll just have to leave them to fight over the bucket."

You put the bucket down and one of the piglets catches the scent and scampers over, soon surrounded by the others.

"That's enough for you," you say, lifting a protesting and particularly greedy piglet away from the bucket to give others a chance at feeding. You don't look up but you know she's watching and that she approves. The runt of the litter struggles to wedge itself between two larger piglets. You lift it up and make a space for it to feed, ignoring the indignant squeals from its larger neighbours.

"Thank you," says Berenice quietly, once the piglets have knocked the bucket over and eaten everything. "Would you like some lunch? We'll be eating soon."

"I haven't had breakfast yet. I'd better be getting back." You're about to leave it there before you add, "I've got some good news to tell my mother."

"Oh?" she smiles invitingly.

"Rufus wants me to join him on his boat."

"Phin, that's wonderful," she says, and the smile lights up her eyes. "You'll be putting those strong shoulders to good use."

You blush and then blush deeper because you know you're blushing, but she's kind enough to turn her attention to the bucket, wiping the wooden handle with the hem of her tunic so it's clean for you to hold.

At home, your mother and Timaeus have retreated to the cool interior of the windowless living room where they sit on a reed mat in a pool of light coming in from the open door before a cloth spread with bread, goat's cheese, cucumbers and olives. "Tim tells me you have news," says your mother, looking up and trying not to appear worried.

"It's good news," you say, but she still remains tense. "It is. Rufus wants me to join him on his boat."

"As a fisherman?" she asks.

"Yeah," you laugh. "What else?" You stare at her, willing her to smile, and gradually the tautness about her relaxes a little.

She looks up as fear and joy war within her and then spits on her heart to keep the Evil Eye at bay. "Well, it's not much, but at least it is something," she says loudly to the room in general, hoping that this declaration will fool the Eye and prevent disaster from striking. "Still, I suppose we should be grateful," she continues loudly, but shoots you a conspiratorial look of pride before coming up behind you, squeezing your shoulders tightly and planting a kiss on your forehead. "You'll need protection," she whispers, "my clever boy."

She reaches behind one of the clay pots she uses for mixing dough, and pulls out a small pouch of coins that *he* still hasn't discovered and drunk. "I'll need a live chicken," she says. "If you eat up quick, you can get to the market for me."

Outside, despite a breeze stirring, the air still feels unbearably hot and close and it's not long before your tunic clings to you. The sun is a hazy grey orb and the air has filled with dust, which is not good for the drying strings of fish that you and Timaeus duck under as you make your way out of the courtyard.

We lose interest in you and flit through houses in search of anything that might feed us. A lot of people sleep through the heat of the day. We find two sisters arguing heatedly over something trivial. Hardly a meal there. Then in one of the inner rooms a husband forces himself upon his wife, and as he straddles her, she cries out and wakes their sleeping baby. There is an old woman who struggles to breathe as she lies on her mat wheezing. Her daughter-in-law holds her hand and prays silently. We pause there for a moment, but it's soon evident to us that the woman won't be dying today.

With you and Timaeus busy in the market, your mother takes a lamp around to a neighbour who is rendering pig lard, and lights it from their fire. Back home, she places it before the statue of the goddess set into an alcove in the living room wall. She prays fervently for you, finally snuffing out the lamp and smearing ash from the wick onto her forehead. If your family lived in one of the ten towns, instead of this village, she'd spend most of her time in the actual temples. Instead, she must limit her devotion to roadside shrines, house idols, talismans and amulets.

She checks the hazy sun beginning its descent, and hurries down to the bay where the boats are now all beached, the nets dry and the place deserted. She pulls out the knife she's brought with her and pricks a finger with it, squeezing to make blood bead up. She then begins her rites and prayers for your protection from the water, squeezing drops of blood into the Great Lake as her offering. The wind is picking up and a larger wave soaks her. This is not a pleasing omen. She lifts the front of her tunic and spits on her heart to ward away evil.

This draws more of us back towards her. She hurries home, passing under the clusters of thorn bushes and starfish that already dangle above your lintel to keep spirits away. She fetches an old, empty perfume bottle from her dowry and fills it with sea salt, hanging it there also. What she doesn't realize is that instead of repelling us, we're attracted by all this paraphernalia. It tells us: here is a house where fear resides.

And we love fear.

Next, she takes the last of her coins and pays a visit to an old woman who makes amulets and who lives further up the hill, stopping to pray at a small shrine to one of the gods along the way.

She arrives back home at the same time as you. You're clutching a newly purchased chicken upside down by the legs. It protests feebly. Your mother appraises the chicken briefly. It's old and stringy, with its egg-laying days long gone. Your mother shrugs. It's the blood not the meat that she really needs.

More of us wheel overhead, entering the room behind her, attracted by what's about to happen. She takes the chicken, which squawks during the handover, and places a clay bowl before the goddess statue, whispering incantations before severing the chicken's throat, holding tightly as the chicken flaps and struggles, aiming the flow of blood into the bowl. We feast on the chicken's pain and panic – as much as mere animal misery can be called a feast.

Once the chicken is dead, your mother bathes the statue in the blood, offering up prayers and then calling you over and placing her palm in the warm blood, then printing it onto your forehead. She draws back to look at her handiwork, checking that all five fingers have made an imprint.

"The hand of Miriam," she says. "It's powerful protection." Then she plucks a feather from the dead bird, dips it into the blood and flicks it at you, praying with each flick, "The mother's protection from the water, the mother's protection from the waves, the mother's protection from the wind, the mother's protection from the storm, the mother's protection from the spite and jealousy of man."

Timaeus watches solemnly, until you're all distracted by a noise outside. The wind has picked up and a reed roof mat outside that's nailed onto a wooden frame to make a shaded canopy has blown free. We love a good storm and spiral outside, revelling in the wind and the scurrying of people below as they take bedding down from their flat roofs, collect drying fish or apricots to deposit them indoors before the first drops of rain come. You and Timaeus unstring the drying fish and hang them from the ceiling beams of the indoor room. It makes the room feel even more cramped, and the smell is powerful.

Timaeus lights lamps inside as the room is completely dark once the door has been shut. You help your mother pluck the chicken. It's women's work really, but with no sisters, and no one else around to comment, you don't mind. Every now and then your mother bats your hand away as you try to rub at the drying blood on your forehead, which itches. Timaeus sits beside the alcove near the lamp, carving something.

"It's a good job they had such a large haul last night," you say. "There's no way anyone is going out tonight in this weather."

Once the chicken has been plucked, cut up and placed in the cooking pot with spices and a few vegetables, your mother turns her attention to you once more.

"I have a gift for you," she says, her eyes beaming with pleasure. "It's to keep you safe."

She draws out a thin leather strap. In its centre is a small triangle made of bone. Carved into it is an eye.

"Mother, you didn't need to do this," you protest. "How much was it?"

"Don't need to think about that," she says, tying the amulet around your neck. "You're my firstborn. Nothing is too much to keep you safe."

Timaeus looks as if he wants to protest that neither of you is safe as long as *he* is around. You give him a look and he's silent. "What are you carving, anyway?" you ask.

He holds it up. "I know you can't really tell what it is yet," he says, "but it's going to be a phallus. They're meant to be really powerful protection."

"A phallus?" you say, taking a closer look and trying not to smirk. "Whose are you basing it on?"

"I told you, it's not finished," Timaeus bridles.

"And it's tiny," you say, sniggering.

"It's not meant to be life-size," he says, getting annoyed.

"Seriously, thank you. It's a tiny little reminder of you." You laugh even as he punches you. Your mother can't help but smile.

"I can't believe I try to do something nice for you and all you do is make rude comments," he says in mock anger, straddling you and trying to pin down your arms. You're easily strong enough to shake him off, but you don't.

"No, I'm really grateful, Tim; it's what I've always wanted. How could I have even considered fishing without a phallus?"

He keeps punching you, but by this time he's trying not to laugh as well. Even your mother, who wouldn't usually make light of something as important as spiritual protection, can't keep the warmth out of her voice as she tells you both to cut it out; an unfortunate choice of phrase that simply makes you both laugh harder.

It's unbearable and we would have left long ago in search of strife but, like we said earlier, we know who's been making his way back to the village; who has just entered the courtyard now, having beaten his poor donkey steadily for the past two hours, determined to get back before the rain, and almost succeeding. He's wet, and tanked up on several skins of cheap roadside wine. He doesn't stop to tether the donkey; one of you can do that for him. He just lurches against the door, crashing it open. He's in a foul mood.

The laughter dies suddenly. You all disappear inside yourselves like a family of startled tortoises. Your faces become masks of inexpression. Timaeus climbs off you and takes a seat beside you on the mat in one fluid movement.

None of you will meet his eye. Sometimes this power makes him feel good, but even he realizes that it simply masks your communal dislike of him. This feeds his ever-present sense of grievance. It tastes wonderful.

"Well, good to see you too," he slurs sarcastically, and slams the door shut. Aqub – your stepfather of sorts – is back.

Chapter Two

"Am I interrupting?" Aqub sneers, wiping his rain-spattered face with a damp sleeve, and ducking to avoid the strings of drying fish. His eyes flit to the pot. He can smell the chicken cooking. "Meat, eh? What's the occasion?" He glances at your mother. "Or did you have one of your premonitions that I'd be coming home?"

"Welcome back," she says woodenly. "Boys, see to the donkey, and fetch your father some water for his feet."

He notices you bridle when she calls him *father*. "Go on, Timaeus," you say quietly, and Timaeus gratefully slinks out. You won't leave Aqub alone with your mother when he's like this.

"What's been going on?" he says, grabbing you roughly with one of his huge hands, smudging the caked blood with the other.

"Don't!" your mother implores, which makes him chuckle. We're enjoying this too. "It's for protection. Rufus offered Phineas a place in his boat."

"Did he, now?" says Aqub in mock appreciation. "How very generous of him." He turns to you, speaking close enough for you to feel his spittle. "I hope you thanked him politely but

21

reminded Rufus that you already have a job?" He gets closer and growls, "You're a fish salter. *My* fish salter."

"I –" you start, but your mother interrupts.

"Let your father sit down and have his supper." She tries to sound cheerful. "We can talk about all this later."

"What's to talk about?" says Aqub, but comes and sits down just as Timaeus brings in a basin of water. Aqub rinses his hands with it but has forgotten about his mud-flecked feet. Your mother ladles out a generous bowl of stew and tears him some flatbread to go with it, hoping hot food will put him in a better mood.

"Fetch me some wine," Aqub snaps.

You glance at Timaeus. "We've run out," you say.

"Then go and buy some." He pulls out a bone from the stew and gnaws on it.

"With what?" you ask.

He looks up. He really wants a fight. We do love him. "So you've got enough money to live off chicken the moment my back's turned but now, when all I want is a well-earned drink, it's just… gone?" He's missed bullying you. "Get out. Tell Procorus at the tavern I'll pay him tomorrow."

"You still owe him for last time and the time before," you say evenly, and duck quickly as a clay tea bowl whizzes past your head and smashes against the wall.

"Just get me some wine! I don't care whose tab it's on," Aqub shouts. "Can't a man enjoy a welcome home drink?"

You're still crouching, but then you straighten and interrupt our feeding, surprising everyone in the room, not least yourself.

"Home?" you say and hold his gaze. "This isn't your home." We're not sure if it's new-found confidence in your ability to earn, or if you've just finally reached the end of your tether.

Everyone freezes for a moment. This is new.

"What did you say?" Aqub asks quietly. It's like that barely audible growl a wild dog makes before it attacks.

"Off you go, Phin," your mother says, hurriedly ladling out more stew into Aqub's bowl, trying to keep her hands from shaking. "I'm sure the tavern can wait until tomorrow for payment."

She gasps as Aqub flings her arm away and scalding hot stew splatters across her face and arms. We knew this feast would be worth waiting for.

For a fat man, Aqub is remarkably quick on his feet and in a moment he has you pinned by the throat against the wall, lifting you up on tiptoe as you choke and splutter. "I'm sorry? What's that?" he says. "Is that an apology?" He looks up and grabs one of the strings of drying fish with his free hand. "You think you can just go off fishing, eh?" He wraps a string around your neck and pulls hard.

Timaeus is standing paralysed with fear, unsure what to do. As you choke, your arms scrabble against the wall and then a hand flails against the alcove and touches the stone statue of the goddess, almost toppling it over. You don't have time to think, but close your hands around it and strike it as hard as you can against Aqub's head.

He howls, we whoop with joy, and the statue cracks. He drops you, clutching at his temple, blood seeping through his fingers. You retch and cough, grasping your throat and trying to untangle the string around your neck. You should have run.

"Quickly, out," your mother cries, as Timaeus bolts for the door. You lunge forward but hear a ripping sound as Aqub clutches your tunic and yanks you back. He grabs your arm in his meaty fists and brings it down backwards over his knee. There's an audible snap and you gasp, unable even to scream as a wave of pain threatens to engulf you. There's a bulge where the broken bone threatens to burst through your skin. You look up and see a fist raised but then a clay bowl crashes over Aqub's head and he bellows as boiling stew scalds his scalp.

Timaeus grabs you and hauls you out of the door, into the driving rain. He tries to block the door, but Aqub flings his whole weight at it. It splinters and he sprawls at your feet, startling the donkey that Timaeus never got around to tethering. It kicks him hard in the head.

"Run!" your mother shouts, above the wind and the rain, and together she and Timaeus drag you out of the courtyard and onto the street. You scream and then retch when Timaeus touches your broken arm, trying to help you along.

"I'm sorry," he yells, weeping, but you're in too much pain to respond. "Mother, should we go to Antigona's?" She's given you refuge in the past.

"No, that's where he'll come looking," she says. "I've had enough. This ends tonight." She hurries up the narrow cobbled street that leads to the water square; muddy water pours over your bare feet, and your tunic hangs off one shoulder, where it ripped. You arrive at the square where an aqueduct pours water into a stone trough from a spring further up the hills. Water spills over it and down an array of stone channels to irrigate courtyard gardens. Not that they'll need it tonight. None of you are wearing cloaks and you're soon sodden, your teeth chattering from shock as much as cold.

"Is he following?" your mother asks. Welts from the scalding soup begin to redden across her face. "Tim, go and look!"

Timaeus goes and checks but the street is entirely deserted. Who would be out in this weather?

"Mother, we need to get Phin help," says Timaeus, trying to keep the panic out of his voice. You cradle your broken arm with the other, and then vomit. This just aggravates the pain in your throat further, where Aqub bruised your windpipe. We surround you, lapping at your pain like kittens at milk. "Mother, where should we go?" Timaeus pleads.

Your mother holds up a hand to stop him. She's thinking furiously. "Tim, go back, but don't go home. Go to Antigona and tell her what's happened. Tell her not to answer the door to Aqub and that I'll come for you tomorrow."

"But what about you and Phin?" he asks.

"Just go! Let me worry about Phin."

"I'm not leaving you."

"Do as I say. Go! I'll take care of Phin."

"Phin?" Timaeus looks to you. You don't know what your mother is planning, but you just nod; it hurts too much to talk. Timaeus is still not sure.

"Did you hear me? I said go!"

He can barely wrench his eyes off you as he backs away, but eventually he turns and skids back towards Antigona's house. Your mother is still breathing heavily from the exertion and everything else. She slows her breathing down and you sense that she's come to some sort of decision. "I was so worried about protecting you from the waters, I didn't even see the danger before my very eyes," she says, almost to herself. Then she holds your gaze. "This will never happen again as long as I draw breath. I will get you the protection you need. Be strong for just a little longer."

Through the haze of pain you try to ask her where she's taking you, but it's too hard, so you nod as she puts her arm around you and tries to help you hobble forwards. At the water trough she turns, following the aqueduct up towards the hills. You leave the village behind, stumbling upwards along a muddy path flanked with pines and cypress trees. You're both injured and soaked but your mother has never looked more determined. There's a fire in her eyes and she doesn't let you stop.

We suddenly realize where she's taking you. This was a bold move we didn't see coming. We flip and turn in joyful anticipation. Some of us return to the village to summon the others. No one will want to miss this. If you weren't so close to passing out, you might remember the other time you travelled this road, with Justus and another boy from your street, each trying to scare each other with stories of the Teller. It was a hot, sunny day and the dare sounded easy at the time, but once you neared his hut, you could feel it in the air; that sense of danger to the soul. It was you who laughed weakly and said that you'd promised your mother you would run a few errands and needed to get back. The other two, relief flooding their faces, couldn't wait to join you as you all ran as fast as you could away from that place.

Eventually you arrive at the Teller's rundown stone hut. It's surrounded by a low, broken stone wall and a tiny shed from which you hear the mournful bleating of a goat. Light glimmers through cracks in the hut door and your mother glances at you, gathers herself together and then marches forward, pounding on the door loudly. By now there are countless numbers of us wheeling in a large circle around the hut. We can hardly wait.

An unkempt man with missing teeth opens the door, standing silently out of the rain but not inviting you in.

"Please, we need your help," says your mother.

"What is your payment?" he asks.

"You can see my boy is in a bad way. I can bring you money tomorrow."

The man moves to shut the door on us. "Wait," she says. "We have nowhere else to go."

The man shrugs, uninterested, and is about to close the door, but your mother wedges her foot inside. "Listen, I have payment."

He pauses, waiting for more. She glances at you, hoping that through the fog of pain you won't remember this. In a low voice she says, "The night is cold. You'll be wanting someone to keep you warm."

He appraises her, tunic clinging to her ribs. She might be a little old and thin, he's probably thinking, but when the lamps are out, what does it matter? He doesn't look like the kind of man who gets many offers. Nodding, he stands aside for you both to enter.

The hut has a packed earth floor, turning to mud beside the door where the rain leaks in. There's a rough wooden table against one wall, covered in stone jars, scrolls, talismans, and effigies of every kind of god and goddess. Bunches of herbs, thorn bushes, dried starfish and snakeskins hang down from the roof beams. He leads you beside the fireplace and lays you down on a ratty-looking sheepskin.

You're shaking, and we jostle around you, like those piglets around your bucket, feeding on your pain.

"You hurt as well?" the Teller asks, turning to your mother.

She shakes her head, so concerned for you that she doesn't seem to feel her own welts.

"Bite down on this," he says, turning to you and putting a piece of leather in your mouth. You've barely had a chance for fear to register before he snaps your arm back into position. You arch your back in agony, your scream muffled. We gorge ourselves. He turns to your mother. "What is it you want for him?"

"Protection," she says. "The most powerful sort. This must never happen again."

"Who did it?" asks the man.

"A man," she says. "The man who lives with us. I would kill him myself if I had the strength."

The Teller nods, staring at you. "You cannot be in here when it happens," he says without looking at her. "Go into the other room and get the bed warm."

She looks around, and notices an old piece of felt hung over a doorway that must lead to the bedroom.

"Do you have a spare lamp?"

He points at one in an alcove. She twists its wick and lights it from the fire. "Please, take care of him. Do whatever you must." She kisses your forehead lightly.

He kneels beside you, ignoring her, bringing his face close to yours. "I need your name," he says.

You manage to whisper. "Phin. Phineas."

"Phineas what?"

"Phineas, son of Alpheus."

He nods. That's all he needs. He throws a log on the fire and then sets to work. First he positions gods and other statues around you, drawing lines with a chunk of chalk that link and crisscross between them. He makes a small nick in your good arm, dips a feather into it and writes incantations with your blood onto a scrap of parchment. He says words over it, but you barely notice as you slip in and out of consciousness. He lifts your head, lights the parchment and tells you to inhale the smoke.

We know what he's doing and if you could hear us, the noise would deafen you. We whirl and shriek, cartwheeling in frenzied anticipation. Already the walls of your soul have begun to weaken.

Then he squeezes out a few more droplets of your blood and smears them on each of the effigies. One of them he binds in rags and ties around your neck as he continues his incantations. You sense that something is wrong, but luckily for us you're too weak to protest.

He takes a knife to his own arm, bleeding a few drops into a bowl of something liquid, adding pinches from several different jars, plucking a few herbs, which are thrown in along with a desiccated snakeskin, which he crumbles into the mixture. He pours it into a blackened pot over the fire and stirs, his voice rising in volume above the wind and rain outside. We crow with delight. The walls are almost down.

Finally, he makes you sit up and inhale steam from a ladle of the potion. He continues his incantations in a language you don't understand, but this time makes you repeat them. Foolishly, you do. Then he tells you to drink the lot. You manage only a few swallows before you retch them back up, coughing uncontrollably. You can't stop the coughing and scrabble for help as, for the second time that night, your face turns a breathless red.

You can hear your mother next door praying to the gods and sobbing. The walls of your soul fall away. You look up, your face turning a darker shade of red, and then you draw a deep, ragged breath. With screeches of delight we rush inside you, every last one of us. You keep gasping for air for a few moments and then your eyes roll back and you collapse on the sheepskin as if dead.

We have just found ourselves a new home.

Chapter Three

"Phin?" Your mother shakes your shoulder gently. Her face is drawn with worry. "Phin?"

You squint against the sunlight pouring through the doorway. You're not sure where you are, but you can feel inside that something isn't right.

"What happened?" you ask groggily.

"Do you remember anything?"

You try to get up, but your mother pushes you gently back onto the sheepskin. "Shh, just rest. You've been badly hurt."

"No," you say. "Help me up. I need to pee." You stretch out a hand to her and she gasps. There's no sign of injury; none at all. She runs her fingers over your arm and, when you don't flinch, she probes a little, searching for the break. Then she moves your head from side to side, examining your neck. The bruising is gone. "What happened to you?" you say, gently touching a welt on her face from last night's stew.

"It's a miracle!" she breathes, and begins to sob quietly. "The gods be praised." The statues and effigies have been placed back on their shelves and she turns to them, bowing and weeping and thanking them for their mercy. She doesn't realize that it was us

Chris Aslan

that did this. We fixed you up. We live in you now. We're not quite free to take over yet, though. There's still a debt we owe that must be settled. You may not have understood the words you repeated last night, but a deal has been struck and we will keep our side of it. Then you must keep yours.

You walk outside, stiff after falling asleep in wet clothes, and scan the rundown yard. Over by a section of intact wall is a makeshift latrine with a ragged cloth draped in front of it. The rag moves and the man emerges.

"He's cured," your mother cries. "How can I ever thank you enough?" She runs over to him and falls at his feet, uttering prayers of blessing and words of gratitude. He's still standing there uncomfortably after you've taken your turn in the latrine. She can't stop smiling and crying. "The gods have saved you, my darling boy!" she says, and won't stop running her fingers through your curls. "I thought I'd lost you!"

"We should go back," you say gruffly. We couldn't agree more. Until that last debt is settled we live in you, but we still have no control.

You nod to the man and summon your mother with a move of your head. She's left nothing inside the hut. "Are you hungry?" she asks, trotting behind you as you stride purposefully towards the village.

You shrug. Your mind is on other matters.

"Phineas," she says, and you turn around. She pauses, unsure how to continue. "Is everything all right? I thought... I thought you'd be happier."

You shrug. "I just want to get back."

"Yes," she says, "Timaeus will be worried." You're about to head on. "Wait," she says. "Shouldn't we talk about what happened? And what's going to happen next?"

"What's there to say?" You pick up the pace as your mother hurries behind. The empty flat roofs are clustered together as the village comes into view below you. Beyond that, the waters of the Great Lake are still a little choppy, but the air has a freshness after the storm.

At the stone water trough, women are filling jars. They glance at you curiously, eyes wandering over your arms, noticing the tear in your tunic. There are no secrets in a village this small, and they've obviously heard about what happened last night from Antigona or one of the other neighbours. Most click their tongues in pity as you pass. No one envies you, but what can anyone do? Tehinah, the village elder, has never got involved in your domestic situation, and no one else wants to. Why risk a beating from a provoked Aqub?

"How are your boys?"

"Is everything all right?"

You hear the women behind you as your mother still struggles to keep up. She says nothing to them, the slap of her bare feet against the cobbles letting you know she's still following. You pass your courtyard door without stopping and head straight to Antigona's, rapping sharply at their door. Berenice answers.

"The gods be praised," she says, relief flooding her voice as she sees you both. "We've all been out of our minds with worry. Let me call poor Timaeus now."

"Stay here until I come back," you say to your mother as Berenice runs off to find Timaeus. "And keep him here, too."

Timaeus comes charging through the courtyard door. He doesn't know whether to be angry, tearful, relieved or overjoyed to see you both alive, and attempts a blend of everything. He's about to throw his arms around you when he remembers your injured arm. Instead, he hugs your mother tightly and fiercely, burying his face into her shoulder and whispering, "I thought I'd lost you. I thought I'd lost you both."

By the time he looks up you've gone.

You enter the courtyard, sidestepping a pile of dung. The donkey is grazing on the leaves of the pomegranate tree. Aqub sits at the bottom of the stone steps leading up to the roof, nursing his head.

"Didn't you hear me last night?" you say calmly. "I told you this isn't your home. What are you still doing here?"

He growls and then launches himself at you.

It's time for us to repay the debt. We sense that you want to be part of this, too. With us inside, you don't feel fear; just anger and a thirst for vengeance. Together, we trip Aqub up. He sprawls on his front and we jump on his back, lift his head by the hair and smash it hard against the paving stones. He moans and tries to shake us off, but we lift his head, higher this time, and bring it down with more force. We do this again and again. We don't stop when we hear his nose break or his skull crack or when the blood begins to pool around your knees. We would happily have continued until his whole skull was pulp, but a voice interrupts us.

"Phin?" Timaeus is standing in the courtyard doorway, his eyes round with shock. He can't quite believe what he's seeing.

You peer around him but no one else is there. You roll Aqub onto his side, splinters of his skull clinging to the paving stones. "That donkey kicked him really hard," you say coolly. "You saw it, didn't you?"

You grab the donkey's tether and drag it backwards until its hooves step in the puddle of blood. You pause and take the ladle from the water jar and drink deeply. Timaeus remains rooted and silent. "Could you ask Mother to make breakfast?" you say matter-of-factly. "I have to deal with this."

We've repaid our debt. Now you are protected from Aqub forever.

You belong to us.

You grab Aqub by a heel and drag him out of the courtyard, leaving a red smear in your wake. You've never felt so strong, so powerful and so in control. Hah! You pass Antigona's house and hear gasps as she emerges, her arm around your mother.

"The donkey must have kicked him pretty hard last night," you say, as you drag Aqub along. The end of your street slopes upwards but stops abruptly because of a ravine, which marks the edge of the village. Aqub's head bounces on the stone steps as you haul him upwards. A stone wall at waist height offers protection from the ravine and it's over this that everyone on your street tosses any rubbish that can't be reused or fed to pigs. You lift the corpse up, even though it would normally take two strong adult men to manage this. Then you flop him over the wall and watch as his body rolls and bounces down the steep hill, eventually submerging itself among the rest of the rubbish.

You wipe your hands on your tunic and sigh in satisfaction, then gather your breath and turn around. A silent crowd of neighbours has formed around you. "What?" you say. "You don't bury a dog." They're silent, and afraid. "If any of you want to wail or say prayers over him, he's down there," you say.

Justus, Berenice's brother, steps forward. "You can't just… do that," he says, still not completely sure himself what he's accusing you of. "What actually happened?"

"Our donkey kicked Aqub in the head last night," you explain, as if to a child. "Ask Timaeus or my mother. They were there. I don't think anyone will be mourning for him."

"But the blood?" says Justus. "It's still fresh." Of course, he'd know about blood, given the number of pigs he's butchered.

You shrug. "Perhaps he didn't die straight away. Or maybe all that rain stopped the blood from drying. Go and see the donkey for yourselves."

Justus turns to his sister, who is also part of the crowd. "Go and fetch Tehinah," he whispers. "Tell him he should bring other men with him."

"The animal killed someone. It must be put to death," says one of the older women. "It is written."

You shrug. "Kill it if you want. You know where it is."

You make to head home but Justus steps forward, blocking your path. He's a little older, a little taller and a little stronger than you, and you used to be desperate for him to like you. Now, he looks at you warily and we let you sense it. He fears you. This is new for you and already you're developing a taste for it. "Stand aside, Justus," you say. He doesn't move and you shoulder into him. Usually this would be cause enough for a fight, but he senses something dangerous about you, and so do the crowd. You walk back to the courtyard, retracing your steps along the red smear that is already drying and turning brown. The crowd keep their distance, but follow behind you.

Back home, you take hold of the donkey's tether, yanking it away from its defoliation of the pomegranate tree. The swollen pomegranate flowers have begun to darken as they turn to fruit, and they mirror the splattered and bloody floor. "Here," you say, offering the frayed rope to the crowd. No one steps forward. "Well?" You hold their gaze but they all look away.

You sigh in exasperation, and duck through the broken door to your living area, emerging with a knife. The donkey barely looks up at you and doesn't notice the knife until you plunge below the jaw, wrenching it outwards and slicing through the windpipe. The donkey is as startled as everyone else, falling to its knees, gushing blood and wheezing, in an attempt to breathe. It tries to raise itself but then collapses, spattering the feet of the crowd as more blood leaks over the courtyard, pooling at the roots of the pomegranate tree.

"You didn't say prayers to the gods over it," says the same old woman who insisted the animal be killed. You glare at her, dropping the bloodied knife with a clatter, and watch her flinch.

The crowd turn as Tehinah arrives with a group of men, including Rufus and some of his crewmen. Tehinah surveys the carnage. "Where is Aqub?" he asks.

"I threw him away," you say, nodding with your head in the direction of the ravine.

"Justus tells me that you claim the donkey dealt him a fatal head blow," says Tehinah.

"Claim?" you say, clenching your fists. "If Justus doubts me, he should come and tell me himself."

"And the donkey?"

"It should have been put to death with prayers, but which he forgot," says that old woman, shaking her head in disgust.

Tehinah seems unsure what to do next. Then he turns to some of the men. "You'll have to climb down into the ravine and examine the body. And Phineas," he turns towards you, "you'll have to come with us. I'll keep you in the cell until we've examined the body." He addresses the crowd. "Are there any witnesses?"

Timaeus stands there silently. He won't lie for you, but won't say what he saw either. Your mother pushes through the crowd, face pinched with anxiety.

"Come on," says Tehinah, and beckons Rufus and one of the other fishermen to escort you.

"Don't," you say quietly, as Rufus is about to place a hand on your shoulder. "I'm warning you."

"Come on, Phin," says Rufus gently. "No one's accusing you of anything. This is just until things get sorted out.'

He places his hand firmly on your shoulder. No, on *our* shoulder. You belong to us now, you're our home and we don't like curbs on our freedom.

Rufus gasps, his head cracking as he thuds against the wall. He slumps down, shock and confusion all over his face. He knows he's stronger than you and can't understand what just happened. The other fisherman grabs at you, but moments later he's sprawled on the floor, moaning softly. You look up and see your mother, horrified. For a moment, Tehinah and the other men look at each other, uncertain. Then they rush you.

We feast on their pain as within moments they all lie at your feet, moaning. *None of these men ever stepped in to help you when you were powerless and weak*, we whisper to you. *All they understand is fear.* We gorge ourselves on your anger. It tastes so much sweeter now that we're inside you.

The crowd parts silently. Timaeus looks as if he's been winded by a punch to the gut. Berenice buries her head in her mother's shoulder, sobbing. You don't look at any of them as you stalk out of the courtyard, except for Justus, whom you punch in the face, knocking him out cold. You walk down another two streets and then turn out of the village towards the place of the dead. You don't look back.

Chapter Four

As you walk, we fill your head with memories of the violence you've just committed; the skull splitting, nose breaking, blood pooling, all of it. We grant you lucidity for a while, letting the reality of what you've done sink in. You regret hitting Rufus, and Tehinah was just doing his job, but you're happy about Aqub. The memory of his murder makes you smile grimly. This isn't really what we were after. We were hoping for more remorse; more guilt. We love the taste of guilt.

We don't need to rush, though. You still haven't realized that we're in control now, but when you do, you'll feed us a steady diet of hopeless remorse.

You follow a narrow stone path which leaves behind irrigated terraces of vines, and trees of olive, pomegranate, plum and apricot. These give way to unterraced scrub with the occasional cypress or pine. Even they eventually peter out and the path cuts through larger rocks and boulders, where lizards sun themselves. It's a barren, lonely place. Looking back, the village is small in the distance. The path slopes downwards, still hugging the steep side of the valley, until you get to the caves of the dead. You know

38

which one belongs to your family. There's no stone protecting the entrance as no one has been placed in there recently. Ducking inside, you see your father's ossuary and plump yourself down beside it, sitting cross-legged. Your hands are still covered in dried blood, but this no longer bothers you. You have other things to worry about.

It starts to occur to you that there's no going back to the village. They will try to arrest you and contain you. Even if you were able to convince them that Aqub died by the kick of the donkey, that wouldn't explain your subsequent violence or your sudden strength. And Timaeus knows what happened. You know how he'll look at you from now on, eyes flitting away when he realizes you can feel his gaze. He'll look at you the way he always looked at Aqub. So, what are you going to do?

You lean back against the rock wall and try to think, but we muddle your thoughts, and instead your shoulders slump and you begin to feel hopeless.

You wake as the setting sun slants into the cave and pools around your face. You're hungry and thirsty. We plan to keep you that way; never enough to die – we don't want to have to leave our new home – but enough to maintain a general sense of misery that we can feed on. The Great Lake stretches out before you, although the immediate shoreline is hidden by the steep rocky incline. There's no path down, but you pick your way through the boulders. At the shore, you squat down and cup water in your hands. You know you're only supposed to drink from springs or streams, but right now you're too thirsty to care.

Once you're a little sated, you start scrubbing at the dried blood, which covers your torn tunic as well. In the end you strip everything off and use your waist cloth – which still smells of fish – to scrub yourself down. By now the sun is setting, you have nothing to wear but wet clothes and nothing to eat at all. The climb back up to the caves warms you a little, but your cheeks feel sunken and your belly hollow. You curl up inside the cave beside your father's ossuary, teeth chattering and belly gnawing with hunger. You try not to think about tomorrow, or the day after that, or how you will survive. "What have I done?" you whisper to yourself over and over again. We feel full.

And so ends our first day together.

When you wake the following morning, you know that you need to think – make some kind of plan – but we won't allow you clarity. Instead, you climb down to the shore and drink from the lake again. Your stomach is cramping with hunger, and then with something else. You scurry behind a rock, squatting just as your bowels gush open. This is why you shouldn't drink lake water. Once it's over, you're still panting from the cramps, and waddle back to the lake to clean yourself up as best you can. By the time you've hauled yourself up to the caves, you can hear voices and you spot people.

It's your mother and Berenice. *Who told them to come? Don't they know who you are and what you've done?* We flood your mind with fear and suspicion. You fight us, shaking your head and trying to get rid of the thoughts we put there. We're gaining strength over you, though, and we keep you wary. You remain hidden behind a boulder as the women call out for you among the caves. You follow behind them, desperate for their company, but terrified of it as well. Berenice catches a glimpse of you out of the corner of her eye. She looks more nervous than happy, making our job much easier. We fill your mind with thoughts of shame. *How could you let her see you like this? Do you think she'd be here if she'd seen what Timaeus saw yesterday? She's only here out of pity for your poor mother. Why else would she be here?*

"Wait," she calls, as you slink back behind a rock. "Verutia, I just saw him over there."

Your mother looks up. You're shocked. How can she have aged like that over the course of one day? "My son," she calls. "Don't be afraid. It's just us. Just two women."

You long to run to her and let her hold you in her arms, stroking your hair and telling you that everything will be all right. But we won't let that happen. She waits, scanning the boulders for some sign of you. "I've brought you some fish and some bread," she says, and waits for you to respond. "And some boiled eggs and some dates," she adds, as if this will lure you out like that feral cat you feed. "Phin, you must be so hungry."

You squat there. *I can never go back* is the only thought we'll let you think.

"Maybe we should leave the food for him," you hear Berenice whisper. There's a pause, and then your mother calls out again.

"I've left the food with a blanket beside your father. We'll come back again tomorrow." They're about to leave – no one lingers by the caves of the dead for long – and then your mother attempts a note of optimism. "It will all be all right."

You watch them move off, but stay rooted behind the rock for longer than is really necessary, your stomach growling in anticipation of food. Clambering back to the mouth of the cave, you see a simple woven basket perched on a flat rock, with the food decoratively arranged. You grab a date, which we let you have, and then start peeling the shell off one of the eggs. For a moment you hold it in your hand; it's soft but firm. You're about to rub it against the salted fish for flavour, but we make you drop it. It rolls down, bouncing on some rocks, breaking into two and landing in the dust. You curse your clumsiness quietly, scurrying after it, brushing off the dirt, dried twigs and goat droppings as best you can, and eat it quickly. Then you pick up a dry, salted sardine, but the same thing happens. You're beginning to realize that this isn't just clumsiness. You go to retrieve it, trying to brush off any dirt on your tunic. You eat it, but you're not thinking about the food any more. What's happening to you? Fear is gently blooming in your heart. We relish it unhurriedly. Let the dawning realization of your predicament happen slowly. Soon perplexity will give way to mounting horror and then crushing despair. That's the plan we have for you over the next few days.

You wake, wrapped in the blanket. The night was pleasantly cool, but it occurs to you that autumn is coming. What will you do then? Your hand flutters to the talismans around your neck. There's the one your mother gave you as protection from the Eye, and then the small effigy, wrapped and bound, which the Teller placed around your neck. You don't want to think about what happened in his hut, but you wonder if it's this amulet that gave you strength to fight off Rufus, Tehinah and his men, keeping you protected. You don't feel very protected now. We start the morning sipping on the fear seeping through you. Last night, you placed the flat basket with the remaining food up in an alcove away from rats, and now we make you flip it. The contents scatter on the cave floor. You know this wasn't your own doing. As you brush off pieces of dried bread and fish, the fear grows.

Thinking simply turns to worry. You sit huddled back in the blanket with a dusty piece of bread in your hand, trying to work out what is going on and what you should do next. You know you can't go back to the village. Your next thought is of running away. The Great Lake is large and there must be other fishing towns or villages where a young man can find work on the boats. A fist slams into the side of your face, stunning you by its suddenness and ferocity. It's your fist. We did that. We're not going anywhere and nor are you. "What?" you whisper, staring at your fist in horror. Then you start to whimper.

You stay there huddled, mewling to yourself like a stray kitten, until we sense people approaching and we drive you out of the cave, jumping from boulder to boulder.

"Wait, Phin," you hear Berenice call out. But you don't.

At the lake, you drink, and squat to relieve yourself. You're about to return to the cave, but we decide to explore a bit. This is our territory now, and we want to get to know it. We walk you along the shoreline. The bay where you drink is barely a bar of sand and grit before the hillside sweeps upwards, but a little further along is a wider cove where a boat could be beached. You climb up from there, arriving at more caves of the dead. Some are natural but most were dug out. We enter into them, running your hands over the ossuaries. Death is a wonderful thing to be around.

Then we take you steadily higher until you've visited the last cave and come up onto the hillside. This is where shepherd boys herd their sheep and goats in spring until they need to be taken to summer pasture. There's not much for the sheep to feed on, although after the rains the pig herders come and let their swine root out fungi. It's a wild and lonely place, and we love it.

Back at the cave, the empty flat basket has been replaced with another, containing bread, dates and a fresh, soft goat's cheese wrapped in vine leaves. You're about to pick it up, but then remember what happened with your other food. The basket is already on the ground, so you bend down, gently pulling away the vine leaves, and try eating the cheese like a dog. You don't think we're that easy to fool, do you? You're as bad as your mother, thinking a talisman or two will keep us at bay. We push your head hard down into the cheese so that you can't breathe without inhaling some of it. You cough and choke as we release you, blowing your nose to get the cheese out.

"Stop!" you say, although you're not sure who it is you're speaking to.

We decide it's time to talk back. You hear our voices in your head. "You belong to us now," we say. "We decide when to stop."

You gasp. "Please, just leave me alone, whoever you are," you say, trying not to let your voice tremble.

"Leave you alone?" we say in your head. "You'll never be alone again. We'll always be with you. You belong to us now."

"Get out!" you shriek, tearing at your hair. "Get out of me!"

You slap at your head as if you could somehow dislodge us, and this makes us laugh. "Get out!" you scream, which just makes us laugh harder.

By the following morning, you've taken to talking to us. It's mainly swearing, occasionally pleading and begging. Your mother and Berenice find you rocking in the cave, huddled up in your blanket and muttering to yourself. "Phin," your mother says gently, but she still startles you.

"Get away from me," you say. "I don't know what I'll do to you." You understand now that we don't like you talking to anyone but us and the dead. We're possessive.

Berenice backs out of the cave warily.

"I said get away!"

"Phin, what's happened to you?" your mother's voice quavers, and tears glass over her eyes. "What have I done?" She moves to stroke your hair, but you hiss at her and bite at the air as she hurries backwards.

"They're in me," you snarl at her. "They're inside my head."

Berenice looks at your mother in confusion, but your mother understands. "I thought I was doing the right thing," she sobs. "I thought I was protecting you." We can feel your will rising up, wanting to reach a hand out to your mother, so quick to forgive. But we're stronger. We snarl at them both and then release a torrent of profanity. They back out, and we raise your voice louder, hurling abuse like stones as they scurry off. In their hasty retreat they forget to leave food for you. You go down to the lake to drink and then, on your way back to the caves, you notice the lizards sunning themselves on the rocks. Some of them are quite large. You sidle slowly up to one of the rocks and we give speed to your hand as it flashes out and grabs a lizard. It has little time to struggle before you've bitten off its head and then begun to chew the torso. Each day you're becoming a little more ours.

* * *

The next day, you've just come back from the lake when you hear Timaeus calling you. It's the first time he's come, and hearing his voice swells you with love for him and reminds you of all you used to be. You hasten towards him until we trip you up. You displease us.

He's sitting cross-legged at the mouth of the cave. When he sees you, he calls out, "Phin!" but doesn't move, not wanting to startle you. "Mother says she's sorry for forgetting to leave food yesterday," he says, keeping his eyes on you and speaking gently, as if you were a skittish wild animal. "It's so good to see you again. Come and sit down here and let's have breakfast together."

You remain where you are, wary.

"Come on," Timaeus coaxes. "Rufus was asking after you. He wants to know when you'll start working the boat with him."

"Rufus?" you say. He's managed to involve you in a conversation. "The man I threw against a wall?"

"That was just a misunderstanding," Timaeus says. Tentatively, you draw closer to him. "Berenice is asking after you. We all miss you."

You draw closer. Something isn't quite right, but you're not sure what it is.

"What does she say?" you ask.

"She just wants to make sure you're all right. We all miss you, the whole village."

The whole village? Why is he lying? As you get closer, you notice perspiration beading on Timaeus's forehead. What game is he playing? What is he trying to do? You stare hard at him, and although he holds your gaze, his eyes shift a little to the left. Too late, you turn and see a blade flashing in the sunlight. He was just the distraction. Your mother has crept up on us and you don't even have time to scream as the blade slices down towards your throat.

Chapter Five

The blade catches on something and you expect to feel pain course through your body, but instead the two amulets around your neck thud to the ground, their leather thongs cut. Your mother grabs the larger one, ripping away the protective wrapping from the effigy while backing away fast from you, lest you lunge at her. Once it's unwrapped, she hurls the effigy as hard as she can against one of the large boulders and the effigy shatters.

She's breathing hard and looks at you to see if there's any change. "Phin?" she says.

Your poor mother really doesn't understand much. It'll certainly take more than a broken talisman to get rid of us.

"We're not going anywhere," we cackle, using our voices. As she and Timaeus hear our many voices in you, their eyes widen in fright. For the first time, their fears have been realized. Something that is not you inhabits and possesses you.

"No!" your mother whispers, backing away. Timaeus grabs her by the hand. They duck as a rock smacks the boulder behind them.

"Quick," Timaeus shouts, and they run back towards the village, rocks raining down around them.

Once they're out of reach, we clamber back to the cave entrance, pick up the flat basket of food they've left behind and hurl the whole thing away from us. Food scatters into crevices in the rocks. We might let you forage for some of it later, or you can catch a couple of lizards, but you need to be taught a lesson. You need to learn that you must never, can never, speak to your family again.

Two days go by with no visitors. You long for them, yet dread their coming. You're desperately lonely, but never alone. We're your only company and you spend much of the time wheedling, cajoling, raging, and pleading for us to leave you. When your mother does reappear, she's with the Teller. Who knows what she had to pay him to get him here? Yet here he is.

We taunt and mock him in a language neither you nor your mother understand. He does, though. We tell him what we'll do to him if he attempts to force us out of you. He turns to your mother and tries to explain the danger and the hopelessness of trying to make us leave. After all, a deal's a deal; you may be hungry, lonely and an outcast, but you're still breathing. We're protecting you and we always will. Your mother pleads with him.

He takes out a nub of chalk from a cloth satchel and begins to draw talismans and other symbols on the ground and on the rocks around us. How dare he? We don't let him get very far. We leap on him, snapping the fingers of his writing hand backwards, breaking them effortlessly. He screams and tries to run, clutching his broken fingers with the other hand as we yell threats and obscenities.

"Ah!" He stumbles to the ground as a stone we threw finds its mark on the back of his head. Your mother helps him up, blood already matting his hair, and drags him away. We keep throwing stones. Were we not clear? We don't like you talking to other people.

For the rest of the day, the air gets hotter and thicker as clouds pile up above the Great Lake. Finally, around sunset, the storm breaks. We love storms, with their wildness and destruction. We pull off your clothes and climb up to the slopes above the caves, dancing wildly as the wind picks up and the rain begins to lash against your body; our body now. We dance until you're exhausted and then continue dancing anyway.

You awaken the next morning to the sound of snuffling close to your ear. You're curled up beside one of the rocks on the slopes while pigs grunt and forage around you, hopeful for fungi. They don't seem bothered by your presence as you stretch and get up. The herd is huge, combining the entire adult swine population of your village and the two neighbouring ones, with brand markings on their ears to determine who they belong to. You see Justus behind them, driving them forward. His jaw is still blue and swollen from the punch we gave him. He looks up and spots you. You're dirty and mud-stained and your hair has already begun to mat. You see him curse silently and try to drive the pigs further up the slope, away from you. You watch him silently and then we decide to give you a treat.

We grab at one of the large piglets that's old enough now to join the adult herd. It begins to protest loudly as we pin it to the ground, and then squeals in alarm as we lift it up and bite down hard on its throat.

"Hey," Justus shouts, but he keeps his distance, unsure what else to do. The pig gives an almost human-sounding shriek as we let go for a moment and then bite down again, shaking your head violently and tearing at the throat until a chunk of it comes away in your mouth. Blood begins to spurt, which we make you drink. Justus, and another youth from the other side of the village, yell at the rest of the herd, urging them forward – not that they need any encouragement. They scamper away leaving you alone with the wounded pig. It's still alive and we keep it that way for as long as possible, making you drink blood while we feast on the animal's pain and on your own powerless revulsion at what is happening. The meat would taste delicious if you could butcher the carcass and make a fire, but we won't let that happen.

Perhaps it was a rash move on our part, although we loved the horror on those pig herders' faces. It appears that loss of livestock motivates the village where sympathy for your plight did not. You're sleeping in the cave that night when they come for you. You awake to pitch torches and spears. Tehinah is there and he's called in help from a handful of foreign soldiers garrisoned nearby. Tehinah throws a fishing net over you, tangling you, and then the soldiers force you onto your front, tying your hands behind your back with a length of tough fishing rope.

They pick you up roughly, taking you back to the village. Usually we wouldn't stand for this kind of treatment, but we decide to let it happen. The whole village needs to learn to fear you.

The foreign soldiers follow behind you, prodding you forward with their spears. Sometimes we make you trip or stumble so that a spear will draw blood. Nothing life-threatening, just fun. The soldiers bicker in a language we understand but you don't. Why must they waste their time with you, when they could be drinking and playing dice? You clearly pose no threat, they say, and they wonder why the village elder is so incompetent. Tehinah smiles nervously and uncomprehendingly at them. He's also wondering if it was a waste of good coin to call in foreign soldiers, given how docile you appear.

As you arrive on the outskirts of the village, people peer from around courtyard doors, and soon a crowd follows you, gradually swelling in number. You're led past the main aqueduct and along a street which winds and then opens up at the village square, where the market takes place. They come to a halt in front of Tehinah's courtyard. Beside it is the single-barred room which acts as a debtors' jail.

Manacle

The crowd gather around expectantly as you are moved to the entrance of the jail. Tehinah turns wearily to address the crowd. "Yes, we've managed to capture him," he says, "but there will be no trial until tomorrow. Return to your homes. The trial will take place here at sunrise."

You are prodded into the jail. There's a bucket in the corner and a tatty woven mat with a threadbare blanket. It's certainly nicer than the cave. They leave your hands bound with rope, and you hear the clunk of a wooden beam being put across the door and fastened into place with a lock. Tehinah peers through the bars to ensure you're secure.

"He's not going anywhere," he says to someone outside. "It's late. Let's all get some sleep."

"Uncle Tehinah," we call him, sounding like you; polite and a little deferential. "That fishing net you threw over me; you will pay."

He scowls and is about to say something, but then just sighs, tired, and decides to head for bed. He will remember your words tomorrow.

We let you slump and then sleep until an hour before dawn. Then we jerk you awake. We stand you to your feet and then lift your arms and, with a grunt, we break them free of their bonds, shaking off the frayed tatters of rope. Then, pressing your back against the far wall, we fill you with strength and you run at the door, flinging your shoulder against it. The whole room shakes, and dried mud from the roof above showers down on you. We run at it again and again and again. In the end, the beam holds but the doorway itself gives, splintering in one corner. We rip an opening and clamber through just as Tehinah appears, awoken by the noise.

He tries to tackle you around the legs but as you both fall we kick him hard in the face, hearing the snap of his nose breaking as he collapses unconscious behind us. We get up and run into his courtyard where embers from last night's fire still smoulder in the outdoor hearth. We fill your lungs with air and blow harder than bellows, setting the embers ablaze. We add burning sticks to the flames and then pull them out, placing them in the splintered jail doorway and we blow until the flames are licking around the door. Tehinah's wife comes in search of her husband, and we snarl at her. She gasps and turns to run, but we push her, sending her sprawling on the courtyard floor, where she moans but lies still. We spot one of the pitch torches Tehinah used last night and plunge it into the flaming cell to light it. Then we run with it down to the bay, holding it aloft like an athlete.

It's almost dawn and time for the boats to come in. We'll give them a beacon to guide them. Down in the bay, the storage hut is made of old dry wood and is soon blazing. The dawn sky is light enough to show up the black plumes of smoke, but dark enough for the flames to burn brightly. We hear shouts from the village above and then calls of anger and distress out on the waters from the first returning boats. Your mother never allowed you to swim, fearing for your saftey, but we know what to do. We shrug out of your dirty, torn tunic, and dive you into the waters in just your waist cloth, swimming hard along the shoreline back to the little bay below the place of the dead.

We emerge from the waters as the sun crests the eastern hills. Looking back, we can still see plumes of smoke. By the time the first boats arrived there would have been little left to salvage and not much point putting the fire out.

We didn't kill anyone, and only destroyed the jail and a fishing hut. We could have done a lot worse, but we don't want to encourage retribution; we just want everyone to leave you alone.

We're all you need now.

At first, our strategy seems to work. Your feet are hardening now that you walk everywhere barefooted. Occasionally you step on a thorn, which we leave long enough to enjoy your whimpering before we slowly draw it out. Your fingernails are growing long and some have split.

Since your family stopped bringing you food, you've subsisted on lizards, and we've also allowed you to roam near the village at night. It's summer and there are peach trees to steal from, vines to rob, and carrots to uproot.

The more isolated you remain, the more ours you become and the more at home we feel. Then, one morning, you wake up as the sun slants through the mouth of the cave and you see your brother squatting silently just opposite you, watching.

"I didn't want to wake you up, Phin," he says softly.

Your heart leaps at hearing your name spoken. Your eyes well up with tears and you sob. "Oh Tim, I have missed you." Your voice sounds rusty from lack of use. You reach forward gently, wanting to stroke his face, to know that he's really there. Instead, your hand tightens around his throat, pinioning him to the cave wall.

"If you leave now," we hiss at him, "you leave without broken bones. Never come back."

"Phin," Timaeus chokes. "Fight them! Remember who you are. I need my big brother back. I love you."

He doesn't say more because we tighten our grip on his throat again. Much as we're enjoying his physical pain, we know this won't be enough to keep him away. We don't really want to kill him as that will just mean more soldiers and possibly an attempted execution, but something must be done to stop him ever coming back.

"You love me, eh?" we hiss, using your voice. "So is this what you want?" We slam him to the ground, winding him, reaching under his tunic and ripping off his waist cloth.

His eyes widen in horror as he realizes what you're about to do to him. How you're going to hurt him in a way that might never heal. He starts kicking at you hard. We move deftly to the side, trying to avoid his legs, keeping him pinned down and tugging off your waist cloth. But it's difficult to hitch up his tunic with one hand and try to flip him over onto his front with the other. This distracts us for a moment and the next thing we know, you're sprawled on top of your brother with a blinding pain in your temple. Timaeus still clutches a rock in his hand as he slithers from underneath you. His tunic rips in a frantic effort to get away. You look up, vision blurred from the blow, to see him stumble away, sobbing.

You lie there long after he's gone. The pain in your head is bad and you feel blood ooze and then congeal from the wound. Much worse is the lucidity we allow you as you realize the full horror of what you were about to do. The worst part is that, although we were in control, there was a part of you that wanted to hurt and to feel powerful and to be in control for just a moment. There was a part of you that was excited.

Now, blended with your despair is a sense of relief. Your shame is so great that you don't want your brother to ever see you again, and now he won't. Not after you've betrayed him in the worst way imaginable.

There can be no coming back from this. It is the last bridge burnt. We put these thoughts in your head and sup on your despair. When you eventually clamber to your feet, your waist cloth lies in the dust. You pick it up and dab gently at your temple before dropping it to the ground. You walk out of the cave naked. What need have you for clothes now? You're not a man. You're wild.

That wheezing old woman we used to watch finally dies and a crowd of mourners come to the caves to bury her. It would be inconceivable to take the dead anywhere else. You watch from behind a rock. The mourners are clearly fearful, checking around furtively. We enjoy their grief and sorrow, but the village will have to find a new place for their dead. As we've often said, we intend to keep you to ourselves.

With this in mind, we send you out to disrupt the funeral proceedings. You swoop down on them, dirty and naked, and begin cackling. One woman faints and others shriek, and the whole crowd begins to surge back. A child gets pushed off the path, falls and begins to wail and scream in terror. You spot a mourner who has travelled from elsewhere wearing a cloth satchel with a couple of rounds of bread protruding from it, and you snatch it. We even let you wolf down the bread, squatting beside the shrouded corpse, abandoned as the crowd beat a hasty retreat. Once they're gone, we let you talk to the corpse, even though it's shrouded and you don't know if it was a man or woman. Eventually you lift it in your arms and drag it into the nearest cave. We don't mind you talking to the dead.

We had hoped this incident might dissuade the village from burying their dead here. Surely they can find somewhere else and just leave us alone? Instead, it prompts your second arrest. This time a large number of village men led by Tehinah and including Justus and Rufus come to the cave, along with a whole section of foreign soldiers. Again, they arrive at night while you sleep, with pitch torches and spears. They also bring metal chains which they bind you with. It seems the whole village is privy to this plan, and the only people you don't see in the crowd that has formed in the market are Timaeus, your mother and Berenice. The shame is probably too much for them. Although it's night, the market square is all lit up with pitch torches.

We notice that the debtors' jail has been rebuilt, this time with a new, much thicker door. We expect you to be taken to it, but instead you're pushed and shoved down a side street to the village blacksmith's. He's been busy. The soldiers surround you with spears, and one of them barks at you to place your hands in front of you. The blacksmith is muscular and imposing, but looks at you warily as he takes two manacles and fits them over your wrists. He uses iron pincers to draw a white-hot pin from the fire. You can feel the heat radiating off it as he fits it into a slot in the manacle on your right hand and hammers it into place. The metal is still soft and fills the hole like plaster. Then he plunges your arm into a bucket of water and the metal hisses and steam rises. He does the same with your left hand. There is no mechanism for removing these manacles; they have been designed to stay on your wrists forever. Between them is a short, thick chain.

The soldiers, feeling more confident now that you're properly chained, prod you and jostle you back towards the market, where the crowd is still waiting.

Tehinah, who has remained with the crowd, steps forward. The break in the bridge of his nose is still an angry dark red. "Is he secure?" he asks one of the soldiers, who nods. "Make sure he's facing the crowd so they can see he's chained."

"Shouldn't we, you know, cover him or something?" says one of the village elders. "Look at all the women here."

Tehinah thinks for a moment. "No, you don't clothe wild animals. Let them see him for what he truly is."

You're flanked by soldiers who hold you secure by your shoulders. Your arms are held in front of you and everyone can see the heavy chain that constrains them. Some of the soldiers wrinkle their nose at your smell. You stand before the entire community dirty, naked and pathetically thin in contrast to the strong, beefy soldiers.

Tehinah steps forward and clears his throat. "I'd like to thank our foreign guests for their help. We are grateful and we are loyal." He pauses, not one for public speaking, but it doesn't matter, as the crowd claps and cheers. "The prisoner will be housed here in the cell until trial tomorrow."

Some of the fishermen from the crew you had hoped to join make fists, pointing their thumbs down, as if this was an arena. They want you executed. Others notice and adopt the same signal. Justus is one of them.

"I understand your anger," says Tehinah, calming them with his hands. "I too want justice, but all in good time."

"Hurt him," says a loud voice that sounds like many voices speaking at once. It scares the crowd into silence. "Hurt him," we say again, using your mouth. "Whip him, beat him, torture him, but you will not kill him or contain him. We won't allow it."

There's a flurry of hushed whispers among the crowd. Even Tehinah is shaken by hearing so many voices utter from your mouth. "Lock him up now," he says to the soldiers.

"We won't let you do that," we say. "Leave us alone or you will be sorry."

"What is this?" snarls the commander, and yanks hard at your chain, causing you to stumble forward. "Come on, boys, get him inside."

The other soldiers can't comply quickly enough. They surround you and they're about to drag you into the new cell, but we're faster and stronger than anything they've seen before. Clasping your hands together to make a large fist, we punch in one direction and then the other with such ferocity that soldiers don't fall as much as fly before thudding to the ground. The commander comes at us and we loop our arms over his head and spin around, garrotting him with the chain. His face turns red as he chokes and splutters. "Back off," we hiss at the remaining soldiers. "Drop your spears."

They look to one another as the commander, still fighting for air, nods his head. They move away slightly and we release pressure, allowing the commander to breathe. One of the young men from the village sees this impasse and runs forward with a battle cry, grabbing a spear from a fallen soldier in an attempt to strike you. We use the commander as a shield and he's about to get stuck with a spear when another soldier manages to trip the youth over.

We release the commander and spin, knocking several more soldiers to the ground. The crowd cry out in fear and anger, but no one wants to intervene. We're breathing heavily, and then with a loud cry we summon all our energy and rip your arms against the chain, straining with all our strength in your skinny little body, until the chain snaps at one end. The crowd gasp and spit on their hearts to protect themselves from evil. With a loud grunt, we tug at the other end of the chain until this too bends and snaps.

"Try this again and we will kill," we spit at the crowd.

Then we stalk off beyond the light of torches, leaving the noise of the crowd behind us. No one follows. As we leave the village behind, we find a large boulder and smash your left wrist down on it, again and again. Once or twice we break a finger bone but we can heal that later. Finally, with a crack, the manacle slips from your left wrist. You lope back towards the caves and there is only darkness and silence and the clink of the one remaining link in the chain which still hangs from the manacle on your right wrist.

Chapter Six

Finally we are left alone with you.

There are the three boys who dare each other to come close to your cave. At first it's just a joke to them, but when they see you, with your wild eyes, straggly beard, matted hair and general filth, it doesn't seem so funny. Then, when we growl at them they scarper, yelling in fright, and don't return.

Once there was a couple travelling from another town who had lost their way. They pass with a donkey heavily laden and stop to bicker about which direction to try next. They don't notice you and we stay quiet.

Sometimes you see boats on the lake below or herders up on the hills beyond the caves with their flocks of sheep, goats, or pigs. They steer their herds well away from the caves, and straggly shrubs now flourish, no longer grazed to the root. These glimpses of people from afar remind you of humanity and your loneliness. You talk to and curse us most of the time, muttering under your breath. Occasionally we respond by slapping you hard across the face with your own hand. Just so you know who's in charge.

The weather gradually gets cooler but we won't let you wear clothes again. We like it when you shiver, although we do let you nest in your blanket at night. You steal pomegranates and apples and then persimmons as the different fruits come into season. Usually it's after dark, but once or twice hunger causes you to stray into habitation during the day. One time you startle a group of women perched on rickety ladders propped against fruit trees. They run, leaving baskets of fruit behind, so you help yourself.

The next day as you approach the furthest outpost of the village, you notice a flat basket laid prominently beside the path with a round of bread and a few apples. You take them, and the next time you go, there it is again. The villagers, it seems, have decided to keep you fed but out of their village. You feel a brief moment of power, but mainly just rejection. So we get fed too.

During the winter months, it's the food offerings that keep you alive as the lizards hibernate. It's usually just bread and a few olives or dates. Perhaps a salted sardine or two. The hurt of loneliness becomes so great that you discover how physical pain can mask it. You begin cutting yourself with rocks, sometimes sharpening their sides by rubbing them against another rock, and sometimes enjoying the bluntness which bruises more than it cuts as you slash at your arms, your torso and your legs. When blood wells and beads around each slash, the physical sensation of pain brings a numbness almost like peace. At first, we're not sure if we'll permit this, but we decide that the physical pain still tastes good.

Some of your wounds get infected. We enjoy making you smear salt from the sardines left by the village for you into your wounds. It's good for them but you whimper beforehand, knowing that it'll sting like hell, so it's good for us too.

Winter brings with it storms. The cave is open to the lake and sometimes the rain slants so far in that you have to huddle at the far end as rainwater pools around you. When the wind howls and the waves roar, we send you dancing among the boulders, full of madness. One time we plunge you into the waves and make you swim through each trough and crest, spluttering and choking as the waves slam into you. We decide that this is reckless. After all, you're our host and we're here to protect you, so it only happens the once.

You're huddled under your blankets just after dark when another section of foreign soldiers arrives. We don't recognize any of them, and we're tiring of these attempts to contain us. "What do you want with us?" we ask them in their own language, using our many voices. This causes even the fiercest of them to murmur for help from their favourite god.

The commander ignores you. "Kill him," he says to his men, and then they charge. They manage to get a chain around you, but we break it and then we break them. Soon soldiers are sprawled around the cave, crawling for cover as we punch and kick. We even use the remaining manacle on your wrist as a weapon, cracking it down on skull after skull.

Now it's time for the commander. He cowers as we approach him, and pulls out a dagger, which he seems about to use on himself. He's one of those honourable types. We rip it from him and then we tear off his armour and his clothes, until he's naked before us.

We straddle him and flip him onto his front as he whimpers, "Don't... don't rape me. Just kill me and be done with it."

We would happily rape him, but these honour-bound types take vengeance seriously. Same goes with murder. If we kill him, then more soldiers will come back wanting blood. We just want to be left alone.

So, we take the dagger and place the point against his back. "You should have listened," we hiss at him. He wriggles and squirms but we are strong. We look around, counting the number of men fallen. "That's twelve men wounded because of you. Thirteen, if we include what we're about to do to you. So..." we pick up the dagger, "next time you think about picking a fight with us, you might want to remember this." He looks around in frightened confusion and then shrieks in pain as we carve four marks in a row with a diagonal slash through them into his back. We repeat the pattern and then add three more slashes. That's thirteen in all. He faints from the pain, and we clamber off him.

We take you down to the lake and keep you there until well after dawn. By the time you return to the cave, there are brown smears of dried blood on the rocks and in the dust, and a broken sandal, but not much else to indicate what happened last night.

You're unsure how many weeks have passed and you're so unused to human company that at first, when you awake one morning, you think you're dreaming. As you rouse yourself, you realize that it's not a dream and that your mother really is calling your name. She stays a safe distance away, and as you emerge from the cave she averts her eyes briefly, then steels herself and holds your gaze. You can tell that your appearance shocks her. It's not the nakedness; you and Tim often doused yourselves in the courtyard. No, she's never seen you look so dirty, so feral and so scarred and broken.

"Phineas." She swallows, managing to keep her voice controlled, although her eyes still leak tears. "You remember me, don't you?"

"Why have you come? Didn't you listen?" you growl. We don't even have to speak for you.

"Do you know what day it is?" You hear the tremor in her voice. "It's your name day, Phineas. Look, I've got you a present. It's a new tunic. Fine linen. I stitched it myself." She holds it up as a peace offering and takes a few steps closer.

"Don't," you say, and tears splash down your cheeks. "Please, I don't want you to see me like this."

"But you're still my boy, my precious boy," she sobs with a heartbroken smile. "You will always be my son."

She comes closer. How dare she?

"Whore!" we cry. She can tell it's us speaking now, although she still looks as if she's been slapped by you as we hurl at her every invective, every profanity imaginable. It shocks her and she backs off, dropping the new tunic, but it doesn't hurt her enough to keep her away. We know what will. "Whore! What kind of mother comes to gloat at her own handiwork? Yes, you did this to him. This is your doing! This is your fault!"

She stands there weeping, but takes the abuse. "I know," she sobs. "Tell me what to do, Phin. Tell me how I can undo this curse."

We laugh at her. "Is there anything you haven't failed at? You couldn't even stay faithful to your husband."

She gasps. This is a secret she has told nobody.

"Please, don't," she whispers, and it's unclear whether she's pleading with us or you.

"He doesn't even know that Timaeus is only his half-brother," we continue, and your mother staggers back, as if struck hard.

"No," she moans, and hurries away, leaving you trapped inside yourself.

"Whore! Miserable whore!" we shout at her retreating figure as she stumbles back towards the village.

The new tunic she made for you lies in the dust where she dropped it. We pick it up and hold it out to get a good look at it. Your mother is wasted as a fish-salter. Her handiwork is excellent and the tunic would fetch a good price in the market. We tear it straight down the middle.

We employ our usual trick of granting you temporary lucidity so we can feed off your guilt and regret. You kneel down in the dust, too tired and embittered for tears, longing for death. You kneel there for a while and then get up, walking towards the steepest outcrop down to the lake shore. It's almost a cliff. It's only as you use those latent running talents and start speeding towards it that we realize your intentions. Just in time, we buckle you to your knees as you skid along the dirt and gravel, your legs grazed and cut, stopping before the drop.

You don't even notice the physical pain. "Just let me die. Just let me end this," you wail, and then start cutting yourself with the nearest rock for hour after hour, moaning and crying out, long after your voice is hoarse, until your whole body is red with your blood.

There's something we want you to know, Phineas son of Alpheus. We love you. We love you for feeding us.

Chapter Seven

A tooth becomes infected. It's one of your back teeth, and we let the infection set in, swelling your jaw until you groan in agony, tossing feverishly inside the cave. We savour as much pain as possible until the infection becomes health-threatening, and then we reach inside your jaw as you scream at the pain and we wrench the offending tooth out. Blood fills your mouth with the taste of bitter iron, and you curl up, sobbing. The pain gradually recedes and the next day we take a pinch of salt left beside some boiled eggs in your offering basket and we sprinkle it onto the swollen gum. You cry out, but we keep it there, making sure the salt heals the wound. You don't usually get spoiled with boiled eggs, but whoever is responsible for your offering basket must have wondered why you hadn't collected your food for several days. Perhaps they even allowed themselves a brief moment of hope that you might have died.

You've become such an institution that the village have built a pile of stones and an alcove of sorts where they leave your daily food offering. It's out of the rain and high enough so that rats won't get at it. One morning in spring, you go to collect your food from this altar and find, instead of the flat basket, a large bowl still steaming slightly. Bits of pork swim in it among the vegetables and you inhale its rich fragrance. Perhaps today is a celebration or a holy day of some kind. You wolf down the stew as fast as you can, fearful that we might smash the bowl to the ground for sport, or push your head into it and hold you there. People have drowned in less.

You belch and lope off towards the caves. We are concerned. We can sense another power at work within your body; one we can't control. You squat beside the path to defecate. You don't bother screening yourself behind a boulder any more and your scat lies everywhere. As you get up, you stumble, struggling to maintain your balance. The blood thumping in your temples sounds almost deafening and black spots appear and disappear before your eyes. We feel the other power getting stronger, and urge you forward. Although it's early morning and cold, sweat breaks out over your skin and you labour to breathe.

Poison! We shove your fingers down your throat and you retch, resisting, but we keep them there until the stew is vomited up. We fight the effects already working their way through your body. The poison is strong and you should already be dead, but we're strong too. We force you over to a nearby orchard of pomegranate trees beside an irrigation channel. We plunge your head into the waters and make you drink deeply and then we stick your fingers down your throat again to vomit the water, hoping to cleanse you of as much of the poison as possible. You're close to passing out, but we know that the poisoners will soon be out looking for you. With all our strength, you manage to drag yourself over a drystone wall and fall into the long spring grass and thistles on the other side, oblivious to their scratches. You crawl forward, wedging yourself between the wall and some bushes, and then you lose consciousness.

You wake in the night, briefly, and then fall asleep again. The following morning you wake again and try to rouse yourself. Your mouth tastes of death and when you stick out your tongue, it's black. You're very weak, but returning to the caves with no food is not an option. We are livid to think that we almost lost our home. Someone must be taught a lesson. We haul you up with our power back to the irrigation channel and make you drink until your stomach feels painfully swollen. Judging by the sun, it's mid-morning. We can hear activity in a nearby field, where a group of women are planting seed. There is a drystone wall around the field to protect the vegetables from thieving goats. As you enter the gate, blocking off their only exit, the women look up and whiten in fear. "Where is your food?" we rasp, using our many voices. An older woman nods to one of the youngest and she scurries over to a bush where they've hung cloaks and two cloth satchels. "Bring them to us."

She comes closer, trembling, and attempts to lay them down before you. "We said, bring them to us." She's shaking with fear now and trying not to wrinkle her nose at your smell, or recoil from your fingernails, which have grown like claws. Your hair is a matted nest of lice and fleas which bushes down around your shoulders now. "Please, just take them," she whispers, as her lips tremble.

Then we attack. We don't want them dead. We know that will lead to retribution, but we will have some revenge of our own. The village needs to know that when they try something stupid, they will pay.

Soon the women scramble bleeding and weeping back to the village, each of them bruised and with broken ribs where we punched them. We think they got off lightly. We could have done a lot worse.

You squat besides the satchels and we let you eat your fill for once, wanting to build your strength back up. The satchels contain bread and a large goat's cheese with herbs. We even let you take one of the cloaks left behind to add to your nest of bedding back at the cave. The next morning, your altar contains a flat basket of fresh bread and boiled eggs. We sniff them carefully, but we sense no malicious intent, and the food has no ill effect on you.

The remaining manacle begins to rust. It's heavy and it bites and chafes you constantly. We like that.

You lose track of time as days blur and the season changes to summer. Your hair is long now and hangs in filthy matted locks. Your beard is patchy as you've taken to pulling it out when cutting yourself becomes too monotonous. The manacle around your wrist continues to rust. You eat lizards and have become quite adept at catching snakes, too. We manage to dig out a burrow of rabbits and let you feast on their young. The village still leave food offerings for you. No one from the village troubles you. They must have found somewhere else to bury their dead.

Although the village has learned to leave you alone, the foreign soldiers still seem determined to kill you. An attempt is made at dawn one day. These soldiers look bigger and meaner than the ones you've seen before. They rush you with swords and spears.

We bring a shield down on the commander's neck, snapping his spine. He's still alive, but he will never walk again. We knock the soldiers to the ground, but we don't leave it there. Using your teeth, we rip an ear off each of them. "When we return, if there is anyone left alive, we will kill them," we growl, using their language. We take you down to the lake carrying a handful of tattered ears with you, which you scatter in the water. By the time you return, the soldiers are all gone.

After that no more soldiers come.

Your second winter with us approaches and although you shiver at night, you seem to have grown used to this life; resigned to it. Misery and despair have given way to a dull sort of acceptance. By the following spring, we tire of this. We want to taste something different, so we decide it's time for you to visit the village.

We enter at nightfall as families begin their evening meal. We're good at keeping to the shadows, shrinking back if a woman drops in on her neighbours, her stone lamp screened in her hands. Outside your compound, we pause for a moment, listening. Then we clamber silently and swiftly over the wall, dropping down into the courtyard. The paving stones which you last saw slick with blood have been completely cleaned. The pomegranate tree is flowering and the grapevine buds with fresh leaves. Strings of drying sardines festoon the courtyard. You glance up at the roof, where there are more.

We grant you lucidity and you feel a whole range of conflicting emotions. It feels so wonderful yet so awful to be back here. The door to the inner room has been replaced since Aqub broke it. The workmanship isn't very good and light seeps from the cracks around it. You draw closer, peering through a gap between two of the planks. You can only see part of your mother squatting before a cooking pot. You long to call out to her, but you know you can't. She's talking to someone, but you're not sure who. You listen.

"I know you don't like it, but Rufus is being fair. Our household bears a responsibility. We owe the village so much," your mother is saying. "He didn't have to offer Tim the job at all. The gods know, no one else would. Once the damage costs are repaid, he'll be bringing in a decent income."

The other person is silent. Perhaps they nod – you don't know. So, Timaeus is working on the boats now while you live like a tormented animal. You feel the tang of jealousy like bile in the back of your throat. This is good; we haven't tasted jealousy before. But if Timaeus is out on the lake, then who is this other person your mother is talking to?

You try peering through a different crack, but all you can see is the wall and part of the alcove where your mother has placed new statues of gods and goddesses.

"Have a taste of this and tell me if it needs more salt," you hear your mother say, and you put your eye back against the first crack. Berenice comes over, struggling to lower herself as she clutches a swollen belly, and your mother ladles some soup gently into her mouth. It's an intimate gesture, like that of a mother and daughter.

You stumble back, finding it hard to breathe, and knock over a bucket.

"Is there someone out there?" you hear your mother say.

"I'll go," says Berenice.

"No, you stay here."

By the time your mother pokes her head out, we've leapt back over the wall and we're sprinting back towards the caves as you sob uncontrollably. Success!

We fatten ourselves on your renewed misery, letting you cut yourself and howl in anguish. Even though you know it's futile, you keep trying to kill yourself. During spring storms you throw yourself into the waves, hoping you'll drown, but we always swim you to shore. A few times you try dashing yourself with a rock, or jumping from the cliffs, but we've learned to anticipate this and we're always faster than you. We won't let you die. At night, when you howl from the clifftop, your voice carries across the waters. Perhaps Timaeus is out there fishing with his crew as they hear those eerie cries and spit on their hearts to ward off evil.

Summer comes, and with it the violent summer storms. In a way you've come to enjoy them; the wild dancing and shrieking is a brief respite from otherwise crushing misery. One night, a storm springs from nowhere, rousing us from the cave. We scamper along the path to the clifftop and howl in the wind and the rain, letting your hair whip around you. Dawn comes and the waves are violent. As you peer through the rain, you see a fishing boat desperately trying to return to shore. Although the clouds obscure the full moon, there is still a dim light and we cackle at the thought that the crew might drown; Timaeus is possibly among them. The boat is sure to capsize soon.

We spin and yell, working ourselves into a frenzy, and then suddenly the storm stops. It doesn't dissipate or gradually calm; it just stops. In the silence, we hear the cries of the fishermen across the water as they attempt to row their broken boat to shore. They won't be fishing in that boat for a while.

We're not so concerned about them, though. Our senses tingle; senses that you don't understand. Something is terribly wrong. Someone is coming, and with a growing sense of dread, we reach out across the waters. Yes, we feel his presence and his power and he's coming this way.

We howl in anguish. This is our anguish, not yours. We know who approaches and we know about his power. There is nothing we can do to stop him.

We clutch at your hair, tearing at it and shrieking. We can feel him coming closer. And we know we have to get away. We try to make you scramble up the hillside as far from the lake as possible. This is our territory, but if we have to leave it, we will. Anything to distance ourselves from him. We can't bear to leave this place, but we will if it means we can keep you. There are deserts, empty hills; so many places we could make our home. We lift you to your feet and we're about to start running, but *his* power stops us. He's not even close, but already we find that you're walking over to the outcrop with the best view, peering out across the waters and seeking out the speck of a small boat. It's heading this way. We didn't let you walk over there, but you did anyway. What is happening? We sicken as the vile taste of your hope fills our mouths.

We shriek again, slapping at your face with your hands as you resolutely begin to pick your way towards the shore, passing the caves. The sun begins to crest the hills and it's us, not you, who feel exposed. You can see from the direction of the boat that it's heading for a larger bay, nearer the village, and you begin clambering over boulders diagonally down towards it. We want to stop you, but we can't. We're powerless now. We spy a ragged stone blade that you once sharpened. Its sharp side is brown with dried blood from your previous usage and we pick it up, hoping to cut you hard and deep. Instead, it falls from your hands. We howl in frustration. We start to bicker and clamour among ourselves. We've always been united, but this panic is making us turn on each other.

You go faster now, bruising your shins on boulders as you stumble down. You're not sure why you're heading for the bay and the approaching boat. All you know is that you want to go there. Hope continues to kindle and spread through you, making us gag.

By the time you reach the bay, the boat is much nearer and you can see a crew larger than for most fishing boats. One of them, perhaps the crew captain, stands at the prow looking intently towards you.

"But Master, there's barely enough sand to beach the boat there. And it's uninhabited. Let us go to the fishermen's bay." We hear this snatch of speech across the water caught on the incoming wind.

You don't understand the language but you see the man at the prow point towards you, and you do something else that sickens us. You smile.

"No!" we shriek, doubling you over. "Get away, get away, get away!" We're panting and moaning. The pain as he approaches must be worse than anything we've ever inflicted on you. We try to make you bolt into the water. Perhaps we can still swim away. We can't move you. We tear at your hair and shriek.

"Leave us alone!" we cry out, using our many voices. The boat is really close now and some of the men are stripping off their tunics, readying themselves to jump over the sides and haul the boat into the bay. We can even see the whites of their eyes, and none of them widen in fear. We shriek again, doubling over and scratching at your cheeks with your ragged, talon-like fingernails. "Leave us be, we beg you!"

We run at the man closest to us. We don't really have a plan, but perhaps if we attack him we can frighten the others off. You buckle to your knees just before the surf. We didn't do that. Have we completely lost control of you? We try to make you burrow into it. Maybe we can still hide from him and from his piercing gaze. The keel of the boat grinds on the sand as the men haul it up onto shore. Then *he* approaches. We can't stop shrieking, desperate to get away, but we're paralysed.

"Come out of him," he says, and just the power of his words shifts something. We feel your broken will stirring and suddenly it's as if we've been snatched from our stable home and marooned on a boat in the storm, tossed around and struggling to keep our footing.

"Please, leave us alone!" we sob. "What do you want with us?" We beg him, even using his real name; that name by which he is known and feared in our realm.

"Who are you?" he asks us. We're like an ants' nest dug up and exposed to harsh sunlight. We scurry over each other, writhing and contorting, desperate not to disclose our individual names.

"We are Army. There is an army of us here," we say, using our many voices. We cannot refuse him an answer. We know he is more powerful than us, so we beg, "This is our home. Please don't send us out."

"This is not a home for you. This is a man and you will not remain inside him," he answers.

"Please! Have mercy on us," we plead. We can sense his will, though, which remains unyielding, and we realize that there really is no hope of remaining in you. "Listen," we wheedle. "We've kept him safe. We've kept our side of the bargain. He belongs to us."

"He belongs to me," he says.

"At least don't send us far from here. All this…" we gesture, using your hand which still has the manacle attached, "this is our home. Don't send us far away, we beg you. Don't send us into the abyss." We tremble at the thought of the abyss, where there is nothing but us, feeding on each other's misery like ticks on a sheep, without the sheep. We glance up, wheedling, "Show us grace, show us mercy." We dare to hope where we have no right to.

"You will leave this man," he says, and we know that we must. We look around, desperate for a way out, and then we see it. Up on the hillside, high above the caves – our home – we see an enormous herd of swine, led by four young men, combing the countryside for fungi after the storm rains.

"Don't send us far away, we beg you!" we say. "Look, send us into the pigs. Let us stay here. It's our home."

He glances over at the swine, which from here look like countless pink dots in the distance. Then he nods and says, "Go!"

You fall to the ground choking as we tumble out of you in a tumult of terror, desperate to get away from him and his searing presence, and without even time to mourn the loss of our home. We rarely enter animals, because we inspire such terror in them that they often just drop dead straightaway, but now we have no choice.

A ripple of hysteria grips the herd as we enter them. The pigs shriek in that way that sounds unsettlingly human. We have no time to exert our will over them, or to get settled in, because, as one, they stampede down the steep hillside, gaining speed and heading for the cliff where we used to dance and howl when we lived inside you.

We try to stop them, to exercise some kind of control, and we're not the only ones. We hear the impotent shouts and yells of the pig herders behind us, following down the hillside with their sticks, wondering what has possessed their herd. Justus is among them. As the first of the swine reach the cliff they simply keep running, cascading over, followed by hundreds more and then more again, dashing against the rocks below or splashing into the lake, still shrieking, until water fills their lungs. The last of the herd move with the same desperate intensity as the first, until each life is snuffed out and we are left scattered and homeless, fleeing these wild places we love, desperate to get away from him, howling in rage and grief because we are homeless and can no longer remain here. We will never again feast on you, our home, our prize.

AFTER

Chapter Eight

Every muscle is taut and my back is arched as I choke, gasping for air. Then I'm just lying there in the sand, my chest heaving as I try to slow my breathing down. I find that I can. I lift my head up slightly. I can do this too. I can control my body – I'm no longer a prisoner inside it. I look up at a boatload of men shielding their eyes from the glare of the sun as they stare, transfixed, into the distance. Following their gaze, I can just make out a torrent of pink and brown as pigs flow like a waterfall down the hillside and over the cliff, cascading into the lake below. There are three or four pig-herders chasing after the last of them. Even from this distance it's pretty clear their attempts are futile.

I shake myself. Why am I watching this? This might be my only chance. I don't know what's happened to the spirits that were inside me, but they might try to come back at any moment and I can never allow that to happen. While the men are distracted by the pigs, I pull myself up and then sprint into the surf. The pigs have the right idea. I push my body, running and then wading into the lake until my foot touches nothing and my head goes under. I push off from the lake bottom and launch myself forward, deliberately out of my depth. Without the spirits in me, I can't swim and I go under, swallowing water as I go. I can feel the lake bottom underfoot and push off again, breaking the water surface with a gasp. Part of me is still desperate to live, but not if it's the living hell that has been my recent existence. This is my opportunity to be free of the spirits forever. I go under once more and this time I can't feel the lake bottom at all, and start to thrash wildly as my lungs burn for air. *It won't be for long,* I think, and then force myself to open my mouth and let the water rush in.

A muscular arm hooks around my neck and drags me to the surface, clasping me tightly to his chest and forcing the water out of my lungs. I cough and splutter and then gasp greedily for air, eager and weak. I've failed. I try half-heartedly to wriggle from the man's grasp, but he's stronger. He says something in the language of the north shore, and when he sees that I don't understand, he repeats it in our language.

"You're not the most grateful, are you?" He's grinning despite kicking hard to swim us back to the shallows.

"Let me go," I manage once I've stopped coughing. We're trudging out of the water now. I try to push him away, but I'm feeling so weak without the spirits' power in me. I have to get back into the waves. He won't let go of me, and he has a powerful grip.

"Cephas, bring him to me," says another voice, calmer but just as strong, and the man loosens his hold a little. "Come," the other man says to me.

I shrink away from him. I'm not sure why. He looks unremarkable, but somehow I know there's power in him. Maybe it's an echo of the terror the spirits felt towards him. "Just let me go. I have to end this," I croak.

"I have ended it," he says, speaking my language. "They will never torment you again. Look…" And he gestures to the hillside, empty except for the few herders running back to the village for help.

Manacle

"You did this?"

"Yes. I did this. They will never torment you again."

"But how do you know?"

"I know."

Cephas almost carries me as we leave water behind. One of the other fishermen tosses Cephas his waist cloth, which he puts on. Then I notice that I'm naked, except for a large, rusting manacle on my right wrist. I look down at my body. It's a wreck of protruding ribs, scabby with filth and latticed with scars. I touch a hand to my hair, which seems to have felted into one solid mass. I can feel lice scurrying in its undergrowth. The man who saved me – not from the waters but from the spirits – he doesn't seem to see any of that. He puts his hand on my shoulder, gently, and asks, "What's your name?"

"Name?" I'm still a bit dazed. Names are for people, not for whatever it is I've become. I want to explain this to him, but for so long my only words have been curses and I'm not used to speaking to people. Also, I'm distracted by his hand on my shoulder. The last time someone touched me – apart from Cephas just now – it was a hand fluttering weakly in my face as a soldier begged for mercy before I bit off his ear. That was me, or at least them in me. I was a monster. What am I now? This man doesn't flinch at my appearance or wrinkle his nose at my stench. If he knew what I've done... He takes his other hand and lifts my chin so I'm forced to look into his eyes. "What's your name?" he asks again, tenderly.

"My name was Phin," I mumble, trying to look away. "Phineas, son of Alpheus."

"Phin," he says, and tucks a matted strand of hair behind my ear. "Welcome back, Phineas son of Alpheus. Your torment is over."

I look at him and the numbness I feel begins to crumble. "I..." I try to speak, but my voice is husky with emotion and words are still difficult. My vision wobbles and then the tears spill over.

"Oh Phin," he says, and he draws me into his arms. All around me, I feel his physical warmth, his solidity and his strength, and now I'm weeping uncontrollably. He holds me tightly, and whispers in my ear, "It's over. I've saved you. You're safe now. You're free." Which doesn't help, as it just makes me sob even louder. I'm still naked, but apart from the wind against my back, it feels as if I'm clothed, because the folds of his fabric surround me. I picture the people I've loved – there aren't many – and I think about the things I've done to them, and the things I've done to villagers and soldiers, and I feel such anguish. He just holds me fast, whispering in my ear and letting me cry without trying to make me stop. "Phin," he says again, with such tenderness and compassion. I'd forgotten there were things like compassion. I cling to him. I'm not afraid of hurting him like I might have done when the others were still in me.

I don't know how long we remain like this. I don't want it to end. My face is buried in his shoulder, inhaling the smell of clean linen and his sweat. The world is reduced to just me and this man who has saved me from a living hell.

"Cephas," he calls softly, still stroking my filthy hair. "Fetch one of my spare tunics for him."

I lift my head from his shoulder and a string of snot stretches between us. My tears have left a damp patch on his tunic.

"Come, Phineas, let's get you dressed."

I take a step back. I'm shivering now, even though it's a warm day and I'm used to being naked.

"Master, you do realize that he's not one of us?" Cephas says, gesturing at my crotch. Of course, they're from the north shore. *Barbaric, cock-cutting mutilators* is what Aqub used to call them. "You probably didn't notice," Cephas adds, trying to excuse the Master. I've heard that they won't associate with us, never mind allow any physical contact. He holds out a simple linen waist cloth and tunic for me.

"I can't," I say. "They're too clean."

"Not that one. The new one with the blue trim," says the Master to Cephas, who makes a face as if to say: *what a waste.* "And bring the inner-gourd in that same bundle. Our brother Phineas would like to wash."

He called me his brother, even though we're not the same people or even the same religion or language. I'd be happy if he just called me his servant.

"Can you catch?" Cephas tosses over the inner-gourd. It lands nearby and bobs on the lake surface for a moment before it starts to absorb the water and sink.

"We can't do much about your hair for now," says the Master, and then he shrugs off his tunic and walks me back into the water, dipping the gourd and using it to scrub my neck and arms and torso. Black rolls of skin and dirt slough off and my skin turns a couple of shades lighter. He pauses for a moment, and I feel his fingers trace one of the scars on my shoulders from where I used to cut myself.

"I'm so sorry," he says, which is strange because I'm the one that did this to myself.

The other men – and it's a group of at least ten – have got a fire going and have skewered some fish, warming flatbread on stones in the embers. They're not talking much, distracted by the antics over at the bay. Two of the pig-herders have clambered down to where the pig carcasses bob on the waves. They frantically try to beach as many pigs as possible. As we watch, we see one of the other boys running back from my village, a line of anxious villagers trailing behind him.

"We don't have any shears," says the Master. "You'll have to shave and bathe your head in oil to kill the fleas and lice."

"Master," calls one of the men by the fire, and the Master nods and we walk over to the boat.

The Master puts on the dry waist cloth and tunic that Cephas left for him on the sand and then throws a prayer shawl over his

Chris Aslan

shoulder. He passes me the newer waist cloth and a beautiful tunic with a blue trim.

"You should have this one," I say, offering it to him. He smiles and shakes his head. I tuck the waist cloth in place and then pull the tunic over my head. The right sleeve gets caught on the manacle for a moment.

The Master steps back, claps his hands on my shoulders and appraises me. "That's better," he says, smiling. "Come, time for breakfast."

The other men look at me uncomfortably. I wonder if it's because I'm not one of them – one of their religion – or because they've heard that the last time I was with a group of men, I broke bones, bit off ears and paralysed a commander. They say nothing when the Master sits me beside himself on the sand. He tears a piece of flatbread and uses it to pull a sardine off a skewer, which he offers me. Instinctively, I'm about to wolf it down as quickly as possible before the spirits stop me or make me throw it in the sand. Then I remember that I'm free now; that I'm me again. When was the last time I ate with others? It was the chicken stew my mother cooked to celebrate Rufus offering me a place on his boat. This thought gives me such a lump in my throat that I find it hard to swallow. I force the food down anyway. Looking at my bony body, I can see how much I need it.

We look up as a boatful of men and women sail past us, tacking close to the shore. They've left from the fishermen's bay and head towards the narrow spit of beach that really can hardly be called a bay, where pigs are being dragged. A few glance our way, but most are transfixed by the sight of the countless floating pig carcasses. The boat is followed by another and then another. I think I see Rufus in one of the boats and possibly Timaeus, but the boats are so crowded, it's hard to tell. Up on the hillside, a steady stream of people continue to hurry from the village, picking their way down towards the bay where the pigs are.

"Look," says one of the Master's men, curling his lip in revulsion. "They're still going to butcher the carcasses, even though they're full of blood." He shudders.

"It's filthy meat anyway, Yahuda," says another.

The men shake their heads in disgust. I try to remember what price an adult pig of decent size would fetch in the market. They're worth more than sheep or goats, even if these north-shorers won't touch their meat. Pig-herding and fishing are the two main sources of revenue for our village, and every pig from our village was in that herd.

"You sent them there, into those pigs, didn't you?" I say quietly and the Master nods. "How did you do it? I knew they never wanted to leave. They wouldn't even let me kill myself."

"The power I have comes from my Father," he says.

I think for a moment. "Is he a Teller or a Shaman?"

The Master smiles. "No," he says. "He's much more powerful than that."

"I don't understand," I say.

"Nor do most of them," he says, pointing at his men, who are watching the boats unload and villagers dragging carcasses out of the water. "But they still follow me, and slowly, through me, they're learning about my Father."

"Can I learn too?"

"Of course, Phin."

Another boatload of villagers sails towards the bay. But instead of heading straight to the pigs, the man at the prow gestures at his crew to steer towards us. As the boat gets closer I recognize Tehinah at the prow, his brow knitted in concern, his nose still broken.

"Did you see what happened?" he shouts from the boat as it comes closer. "The herders aren't making any sense. They said it was some kind of stampede, but they can't figure out why." As the boat draws nearer, Tehinah and some of the other men jump over the sides – fully clothed due to the presence of women –

and drag the boat up until it's banked. "My name is Tehinah and I'm the village elder…" He stops talking as he notices me. "Get back," he says quietly, and the villagers, following his gaze, need no extra encouragement. "Don't make any sudden or threatening moves; just move away from him slowly and quietly," he says to the Master and his men.

The Master smiles and puts an arm over my shoulder. "Isn't Phin from your village?" he asks.

"Back away. You don't understand. He's not what you think he is," says Tehinah. "Don't be fooled by his appearance."

"I'm not," says the Master, and stands up, addressing the wide-eyed villagers. "I know what was in him, controlling him against his will and tormenting him. You tried everything to get rid of him, but I've saved him from them and sent them into those pigs. They will never trouble him again. His torment is over."

"*His* torment?" shouts one of the older women. "Do you know what our village has suffered because of him? And now this…" She gestures at the scene behind her.

"You saw him when the spirits were in him," says the Master, staring intently at Tehinah but including everyone. "Look at him now. You can tell he's different, can't you?"

I might be imagining it but as Tehinah glances at me, I think there are tears in his eyes.

"He's a curse on our village," says one of the villagers.

"Why don't you take him with you, wherever it is you're going?" shouts another.

Tehinah looks at the Master, sizing him up. "I've heard about you, haven't I?" he says. "You're the one from the north shore who everyone's been talking about. They say you're the chosen one your people have been waiting for. Right? You help your people."

"Yes, and I helped Phin," says the Master.

"But we didn't ask for this." He points at the pigs. "You've helped him. Now, please, just take your men and leave. We don't want any trouble."

"We've done nothing to you," adds one of the women, and others murmur their agreement.

The Master nods. Some of the villagers spit on their hearts to keep evil at bay.

"We just don't want any trouble," says Tehinah again as an explanation of sorts. He looks weary. He takes another look at me, and then mouths silently to the Master, "Thank you." Then, addressing the villagers, he announces, "We're leaving now. We've got a lot to do." The villagers push the boat into water and climb in. No one seems too bothered about getting their clothes wet; they've got more important concerns. They row as well as sail away, whether more eager to salvage their herd or get away from me, I'm not sure.

"At least let's finish breakfast," mutters one of the Master's men. "It took us all night just to get here."

"You're leaving?" I say to the Master, trying to keep the tremor out of my voice as the men return to their food and grunts of conversation.

"Yes. He asked us to go. I've done what I came for. I came to free you."

I smile weakly. "You heard them. I'm a curse. There's no place for me back in the village. Let me go with you. I know I can't repay you for what you did, but I could work with your men. I'll do anything."

"Master?" says one of his men, looking at me darkly. The Master holds up a hand and the man is silent.

"Please." I try to keep the desperation out of my voice but I know I'm failing. "Look, there's nothing for me here."

"I understand," he says, and hope soars in my heart.

"Thank you," I say, and I can't help the tears of relief that well up.

"No, I understand that you think there's nothing for you here in this village, but there is. You have a family. They've suffered too. Go back to them. This is your second chance."

"You heard Tehinah. You saw the villagers," I say. "There are no second chances for me. The whole village hates me."

"Tell them what I've done for you. Tell them of the goodness of God, of his love and mercy. Don't just tell your village; tell everyone in the whole area of the ten towns."

"I want to go with you, Master. Please, let me serve you."

"Then do as I ask," he says firmly, holding my gaze. "I know what it is to walk the path of obedience. It's not an easy path, but I walk it every day. If you call me 'Master' then stay here and speak of me. I know it won't be easy. Can you trust me that this is the right path for you?"

"Please!" I fall at his feet and desperately start kissing them. "I don't eat much. I'll earn my keep."

The other men have put out the fire and stripped off their tunics to push the boat back into the water. Once it's afloat, they hold it there, waiting for the Master.

"Please, I'm begging you. I'll do anything. I can fish or row."

"Phin, it's not my Father's plan for you, and my Father does have a plan for you." He helps me to my feet and kisses my forehead tenderly. "I came here through a storm for you because it was my Father's plan to set you free from torment. I've told you what his plan is for you now. Trust my words." Then he puts his hands on my shoulders, leans closer and whispers a prayer of blessing in my ear.

Something about this prayer calms me and keeps me rooted as he plants a final kiss on my forehead, lets go of me and turns. I'm still desperate to splash through the surf and follow him, to force my way onto that boat if I have to. Yesterday I could have maimed or wounded them all, even if they rushed me at the same time. Instead I stand here, watching as his men haul the Master aboard. He looks back and holds my gaze, nodding slowly. The sail drops and then fills, and the boat begins to move away.

I just stand there as the boat becomes a speck on the horizon and then disappears altogether. I look around. His footprints are still visible in the damp sand. The ashes of the fire where he sat are still warm. I still wear his tunic. But he's gone, and I'm alone, and I don't know what to do next.

Smoke draws my attention to where villagers have piled up the pig carcasses and are now making fires on what little beach there is, hoping the smoke will keep the flies away. They strap poles together to make tripods on which they haul up carcasses to start butchering them before they go off. The villagers are right. I am a curse on our village. Has any individual ever been the cause of so much chaos and destruction? How can I possibly go back? And why would any of them ever want to forgive me?

Chapter Nine

There's nothing for it. I'll have to go home. Can I still call it that? I already know from that one brief foray back that Timaeus and Berenice are now together and that she probably has a baby. The last thing they'll want is me intruding on them. More to the point, the last time I was with my brother I tried to rape him. How am I supposed to face him again? Will he understand that it was them controlling me? Even if it was them at work in me, I was still there. I can never forget the look on his face when he realized what was about to happen to him.

And my mother? I remember some of the names I called her when they were still inside me, and the revelations I received about her from them. How could she possibly want to see me ever again? Perhaps it had been my family's idea to leave poisoned food out for me, so they could mourn who I once was and then move on with their lives. I just don't understand why the Master couldn't take me with him. What's left for me in this village?

I sit on the sand for a while, plagued by these questions. Finally I get up, brush the sand off my tunic and look for a way up the hillside that will lead to the main path back to the village.

I walk and as I do so, I become more conscious of my body. I can feel the scurrying of fleas and lice in my scalp, and find myself scratching the whole time. My finger and toenails are long, cracked talons with dirt deeply lodged in their cuticles. The rusted manacle on my right wrist chafes. Despite the Master's best efforts in the lake to scrub me, I'm still pretty dirty and dishevelled. For the first time, I feel acutely self-conscious about it and even more grateful for the tunic and waist cloth.

I pick my way up through the boulders and scree and then spot the path above. While it's usually pretty deserted, right now it's teeming with people, donkeys and even a couple of camels. Those heading towards the village are all heavily burdened with cuts of pork, hastily made offal-stuffed intestines and piles of swine-skins. Everyone is in a hurry, a race against the heat of the day as they try to salvage and cure as much of the drowned herd as possible before the carcasses begin to bloat and putrefy. No one butchers pigs in summer for this very reason, and they'll be lucky to salvage even half the meat from the herd.

Given the scale of this disaster and my own involvement in it, I decide to avoid the path and the villagers. Even with clothes on, I'm still easy to identify with my wild hair. Instead, I scramble back down towards the shoreline and work my way around until I reach the fishermen's bay. Despite the heat of the day, the bay is also busy as fishing boats ferry piles of swine-skins and pork back to the village. I crouch, waiting behind a rock near the place where the feral cat I once fed used to live. There's no sign of her now. In the lull between one boat leaving and another arriving, I scurry across the sand and make my way up to the village, avoiding the path.

When I get to the village itself, I skitter along back alleys and occasionally hide behind a tree or a stone column as people pass by. I arrive at our courtyard. It occurs to me that no one will be at home as they'll be helping with the salvage operation, but I've got nowhere else to go. I rattle the door handle, which I always used to do instead of knocking. I'm in an exposed position, too near Justus's house, which is a hub of activity as they have facilities for smoking and curing pork and ham. I'm wondering whether to try climbing over the wall when the door opens.

My mother gasps at the sight of me. She rests a small child on her hip and backs into the courtyard, looking around as if to find an exit or a weapon.

"It's me. Phin," I say, holding up my hands to pacify her. "It's just me."

Her lip trembles but she says nothing. I think she's waiting for the many voices to start their mockery and abuse again. I smile, awkwardly. "See? Just me."

"How? How is this possible?" she says, still keeping a safe distance between us.

"There was a man – he comes from the north shore. He has this power. I don't really understand who he is or where the power comes from, but he rescued me. He's more powerful than those things that were inside me. He made them leave, even though they didn't want to. He sent them out of me and into the pigs."

"So the pigs, that was you too," she says quietly, more to herself. She moans, which unsettles the baby. It begins to grizzle. She jigs it on her hip, trying to make it quiet. "This is too much. We'll be cast out."

"The baby," I say. "Tim's baby. Is it a boy or a girl?"

She looks distractedly at the baby and then back at me, and then she gropes behind her, finds the stone steps that lead up to our flat roof and sits down heavily. Her face is white.

I don't know what to say. The silence between us grows. "I wouldn't bother you, except I don't know where else to go," I say finally. There's part of me that assumes she'll protest and come sobbing to take me in her arms, but she doesn't.

So I just stand there as tears brim, waiting for her to react. Waiting for her to be my mother again. She sits there ashen-faced with that baby on her hip, looking tired and old, and I don't know what to do. Finally she turns to the whimpering baby and makes soothing noises.

"Can I..." I take a step forward towards the child and she freezes. "Sorry," I say and stumble back. Of course, how can you trust your grandchild to a monster?

We're silent again.

"You know, I never asked for it," I say, trying not to cry. "I never wanted any of it. It should be the Teller you get angry with, not me."

"The Teller is dead," she says quietly, and uses the heel of her hand to wipe away a tear. "I don't know what to do," she says finally. I don't reply – I don't have any suggestions. She looks up, studying my face. "You know, I used to dream about this moment so many times," she says. "By some miracle you'd be restored to us and when you returned we'd throw our arms around you. The gods know, I prayed for it enough times. But it's not that simple. What are we going to do with you?"

I shrug, and I try to smile as if to say, *it doesn't matter*, but it does, and my eyes won't stop leaking tears.

"We've wept for you so many times. I want you to know that. We tried everything we could think of," she says.

"I know," I say. "Even though they were in control, I still remember everything."

She nods. "I never found out what you did to Timaeus up there in the caves. He wouldn't tell me. You have no idea how hard this has been for him, and I don't just mean what you did, but what they did; the whole village. Every time you destroyed something or hurt someone, he was the one who was punished. I don't just mean name-calling. I mean beatings, people throwing stones at him. It would be someone on our street whose sister was thrashed by you in a field, or someone else who couldn't bury their mother with their father because we had to build a new place of the dead because of you, or a fisherman who'd lost his best nets in that hut you set on fire. Every grievance he paid for. He didn't want me to know, and sometimes he wouldn't come home at all, which was worse because I'd wonder if he'd gone back to you and if you'd killed him. Justus forbade Berenice to come to our house, and when they found out about the romance, they cut her off. Can you imagine? Antigona, my old friend and neighbour, living on the same street and she's never even held her own granddaughter in her arms."

"So, it's a girl," I say, my voice shaking.

"Things were just starting to get better. Tim works for Rufus now – the gods know, no one else would give him work. And that's after what you did to him. It was agreed Tim would work for free for six months to help repay the boat hut you burnt. And those were generous terms. He's always had to be there earlier, work harder, serve better just to be accepted. Now, he's finally bringing in a wage. You know, he brought one of the other boys home for breakfast the other morning. All this time and he might finally have a friend. And then this happens with the pigs. It'll bankrupt Justus. He'll make sure Timaeus pays for what you've done."

"What you've done, you mean," I say quietly. "This was all your doing."

She brushes tears away angrily, but doesn't deny it. "Where do you think Tim and Berenice are? They'll be the last people to leave that bay, even though we only own a few piglets. They'll work extra hard, trying to earn the goodwill of people, trying to be the most helpful, doing the jobs no one else wants to. But once word spreads... There isn't a single family here who won't suffer from this in some way. Who hasn't invested in swine, saving up for a wedding or a boat? And you think I don't know it's all my fault? You think I haven't paid for this? Gods! I keep thinking it will end, but it just gets worse."

I'm beginning to think the same thing myself.

She swallows and her face settles in resolution. "You have to leave."

"Where am I supposed to go? Back to the caves of the dead?"

She shakes her head, not even noticing the sarcasm in my voice. "You can't go back to the caves. They'll look for you there. Once they realize you've lost your power, they'll hunt you down and they'll kill you. If you stay here, Timaeus will report you. What else could he do if he ever wants to be accepted in this village?" She pauses to think. I don't like the way she refers to "my power". It was never mine and I never wanted it. "I'll take the child and go to the bay to help with the salvaging. I'll find Tehinah and beg him to help us. It's about time he took his responsibilities seriously."

"You can't climb down that hillside with a child."

"Who else could I leave her with?" It's an accusation of sorts; no one leaves their granddaughter with a monster.

"And then you'll be rid of me and I'll be Tehinah's problem," I say, hearing the bitterness in my own voice.

Her silence is a reply in itself. She goes inside to fetch some bread and dates for me, and a few sardines. "It's better if you eat these out here." I wonder if she's worried about my fleas, or just doesn't want me in her house. I don't even think of this place as "ours" any more.

I sit down under the vine with the food on a food cloth before me. It's much the same diet as I lived on in the caves, but with no lizards. There is no welcome home, no hot, home-cooked meal. The bread tastes like ash in my mouth.

My mother, a stranger to me now, busies herself collecting food and a skin of water to take with her to the bay, avoiding eye contact or conversation.

"I was hoping," I start, and then wish I hadn't but carry on anyway. "I was hoping you might shave my head and my beard. I can hide the manacle, but this makes me stand out. It'll help get rid of the fleas and lice, too."

"I should go now," she says, picking up the satchel in one hand and clutching the baby to her hip in the other. I still don't know her name. "Wait here. I'll tell Tehinah to knock. No one ever visits us so you'll know it's him. He probably won't get here until sunset." She opens the courtyard door and is about to leave without even saying goodbye. I wish I was dead. Then she turns. "I'll pray to the gods for you."

"The gods?" I sneer. "Aren't they what got me into this hell in the first place?"

She doesn't say anything. She just leaves. I sit there under the vine in a place that was once my home. Even when Aqub was alive, however scared I was of him, I always knew that this was my place and that I was loved by my mother and my brother. I shouldn't have thought of Aqub, because I glance at the pomegranate tree with its swollen blossoms beginning to turn to fruit the colour of freshly shed blood. Of course, I think of Aqub and remember the force in my hands as I rammed his head against the paving stones and pooled them with his blood. Perhaps I deserve all this. I am a murderer, or at least an accomplice to the spirits. I'm a thief, a destroyer; I've dishonoured my mother and my brother in ways that will never heal.

For a moment I consider walking out to the bay until the crowd surround me and drag me to the clifftop, pelting me with stones until I stagger backwards and go the way of the pigs.

Then I remember the words of the Master. I try to commit to memory everything he said. He mentioned something about a plan for me that wouldn't be easy and that I should obey him. I realize that I know almost nothing about him. Tehinah seemed to have heard of him. Miserable as I feel, I'm not ready to finish my life just yet. He won me back. There must be a reason. The Master told me to return to my family and tell them about the goodness of God. Which of the gods did he mean?

He didn't tell me what to do if my family wanted nothing to do with me. What could change their minds? Even if they did, my mother is right: I can't stay here. Not yet, anyway. I wonder if I could adopt the same strategy as Timaeus and somehow make up for all the bad things I've done with good deeds. But what could ever right the balance? What's the opposite of trying to rape your brother, or murdering your stepfather, or maiming and hurting countless people?

I can't let myself think about this. I pull myself to my feet and open the door to the storage room. The shears are still kept in the same place and that's reassuring. I can't shave my head without help, but at least I can shear it. I take off my new tunic and cut as close to the scalp as possible. The hair is so matted that it eventually comes away in one solid piece. I can see the lice scurrying over it. I lift it and quickly throw it onto the embers of the outdoor kitchen fire. The smoke is acrid as the hair hisses and shrivels.

There's a stone jar of olive oil in the storage room and I take off my waist cloth and cover myself in oil, standing in the sun, hoping it will kill any more lice or fleas. Then I take some ash from the fireplace and smear it into the oil, rubbing myself all over until I create a dirty lather of sorts. I don't have a proper scraper but use a knife instead, and scrape off the mixture, bringing dirt and dead skin with it. It hurts whenever the knife goes over one of my scars, which means it hurts a lot. The pain feels reassuringly familiar. One or two more recent cuts begin to bleed again. Once I'm finished, I use some of the water from the storage jar and douse myself. I stay in the sun to dry and take my time paring down the dirty talons that have become my finger and toenails. Once I've finished, I put the tunic back on, and even without a mirror to check, I feel more respectable. I wish I could do the same with the inside of me, scraping away the guilt, shearing off the shame.

I have nothing else to do. I want to look inside the inner room, but I don't. She didn't want me in there. Instead, I sit down in the shade of the vine, staring at the pomegranate tree under which I did my killing. I was dancing through the storm last night and hadn't realized how tired I am until now.

* * *

I'm woken by knocking on the door. I look around. The sun is setting and a cooling evening breeze comes off the lake.

"Tehinah?" I ask, standing on our side of the door.

"Yes," he says. It occurs to me that he could be out there with a group of angry young men ready to lynch me, and that maybe this would be a good thing. I open the door. He's alone.

He looks at my scalp and nods in approval. "Most of the village are still down at the bay. There'll be good fishing around there for the next few days with all that blood and offal in the water." He hands me a prayer shawl like the one the Master wore over his shoulder. "Cover your head with it," he says. "Hopefully everyone will be too busy to notice you, but we can't risk it."

"I oiled my head, but still, I might have fleas," I say with a helpless shrug towards the prayer shawl.

He shrugs. "You can keep it. What am I going to do with it?"

"I'm really grateful –" I start, but he holds up a hand. He doesn't want to hear it. I close the courtyard door behind us without looking back.

We keep to the side streets but we needn't have bothered as there's no one around. The market square feels particularly eerie with no one there. I look around, remembering the last time I was here.

"Is your wife at home?" I ask. "I think I scared her quite badly the last time I saw her."

He shakes his head. "The fewer people who know about you the better. Justus has already sent a group of men to search the caves for you. The people in the boat with me have told everyone else what happened."

He leads me into their courtyard, lights a fire and sets water to boil. "I'll get my shaving kit," he says, and I close the courtyard door behind me and wait.

He comes back with a leather pouch and pulls out a razor, a pouch of ash, and a scraper.

"Is this a good place to sit?" I point to a spot near a drain and take off my tunic. Tehinah studies the criss-crosses of cuts and scars all over me and swallows. "It's probably good that you've got more on your front than your back," he says. "Otherwise people might think you have received the lash or that you're a runaway or something."

"What about this?" I lift up my arm with the manacle still attached.

"I'll see what I can do," he says. He's silent for a moment as he rubs oil into my scalp. "I'm sorry," he says quietly.

"Why are you sorry? It's not your fault. How's your nose?" I ask.

"Are you sure you want to ask me that when I'm holding a razor to your head?"

I think I detect a note of humour. "I am really sorry."

He concentrates on shaving around my left ear and then says, "How much do you remember?"

"Everything."

"I can't imagine."

"My cuts – that wasn't them, it was me. I kept trying to kill myself, but they wouldn't let me."

"We tried too."

I nod. "Was the poison your idea?"

"No."

"Was it my brother's idea?" He doesn't answer, which is an answer in itself. "So, we all tried."

He kneels down beside me and holds my gaze. "This has affected every one of us; every single person in this village. It wasn't our fault either. Now they're going to want someone to blame. It doesn't matter if the pigs were your fault or not. I remember those voices that came out of your mouth, and the way you could just break those chains. I know that wasn't you but whatever was inside you. I know that, and so do the villagers, but right now they're angry and they don't want to remember that."

"So, what am I supposed to do?"

He continues shaving my head in silence and I don't interrupt him because I can tell he's deep in thought.

"You'll have to leave the village tonight. I'll make sure we get the manacle removed. I have a cousin, Rabba, a tanner. It's not a business I'd recommend, but we'll be sending him more pigskins than he'll know what to do with, so he'll need the extra help. I'll write a note for you to take to him. I'll tell him that you're one of my relatives. He'll assume you're from my wife's side of the family. If you thought the smell of fish-salting was bad... He lives at the foot of the hill of the City of Horses near the dyers' quarter. You know which direction that is?" I nod and point eastward. "Take the main road during the night but stay off it in the morning. You can walk in the heat of the day when no one's around and you should get to the city by tomorrow evening."

"Does this mean I can never come back?"

"I don't know. Let people recover first."

I'm quiet as he finishes my scalp and starts lathering my chin and whiskers. When he's finished shaving, he rubs oil into my face and pats my cheeks. "There," he says, taking a step back to admire his work.

"Why are you helping me? I broke your nose. You must have lost pigs today."

"I'm the elder," he says. "It's my job to take care of the village."

"But why help me? I caused havoc in this village."

He seems uncomfortable and avoids my gaze. "This should never have happened. You, your mother, Aqub. I should have taken responsibility earlier. I shouldn't have just stood by and let him treat you all the way he did. I failed."

He pats my shoulder briefly, and then goes into a room off the courtyard to write a letter for me. I hear him sniffing as if he is crying. When he comes back, he hands me a letter and then a cloth satchel containing a skin of water, flatbread, dates, and salted fish. "If you'd waited until tomorrow, you could have taken a whole ham with you," he says, passing me the satchel with a tired smile.

"I still don't understand why you're helping me," I say. "I know it's not just because it's your job."

"No," he says. "This is too little too late."

I think about how he and his wife have no children. He would make a wonderful father, but I don't say this, because who would want me, a monster, as their son?

He hands me a cloak. "You'll need this for the journey."

"I can't repay you."

"Keep it. I can fetch you my spare pair of sandals. They might be a bit big for you."

"It's all right; my soles are tougher than leather," I say.

He looks around the courtyard door to check that no one is coming. A group of villagers trudge up towards Justus's courtyard, heavily laden with cuts of meat to cure. Once they're gone, we head for the blacksmith's. He knocks quietly and then louder but no one is there. I end up giving our village elder a leg up, and he then pulls me onto the wall and we drop down together beside the anvil.

"Why didn't you break the manacle when you still had the power?" he asks.

"I think they left it to remind me that I was enslaved to them."

A large pair of pincers hang on a nail in the wall behind the anvil. Tehinah hauls them down and tries them on the manacle. It's clear after the first attempt that this is hopeless, but he still gives it several more goes before shaking his head in defeat.

"Well, the cloak will come in handy," he says. "Make sure your right arm is hidden under it when you pass people." He wipes sweat from his brow. "Hopefully no one will notice along the way. See if Rabba can take you to a smithy in his city. Otherwise people will jump to conclusions."

"I've noticed people do that a lot," I say. "Will Rabba take me in when he sees the manacle?"

"I've told him enough in my letter," says Tehinah.

I give him a leg up back onto the wall and he hauls me over.

"I'll walk you to the main road," he says.

We walk silently. The cloak has a hood, which helps keep my face hidden. We pass the last house and the stone marker that shows our village limit.

"The gods be with you," he says, and I'm about to embrace him but then I don't because if he flinches it will remind me of who I am.

"Thank you for everything," I say.

"You can stop thanking and apologizing," he says, a little gruffer than I think he meant to, and then he gives me a brief, fierce hug and turns silently back to deal with a village-worth of trouble.

I watch him until he turns a street corner, and then I begin to walk. I pass the roadside tavern where Aqub always owed money. The path feels solid beneath my feet. I walk with purpose. I know where I'm going, even if I don't know what will happen when I get there. The night air feels cool against my scalp, which I keep running my hand over, getting used to not having any hair. Although the manacle still clinks around my wrist, and although my family and the whole village hate me, I feel a curious sense of freedom. I'm no longer a prisoner in my own body. I'm no longer tormented by spirits. I've experienced undeserved kindness from a man whose nose I broke and whose village economy I've ruined. *My Father has a plan for you.* I don't know what it means, but I do know that even without the spirits in me, I'm not alone. I pass the turn off to our neighbouring village, but I keep walking along the main path.

I take the satchel off my shoulder and hold it in one hand with the cloak in the other. Then I begin to run, feeling power in my legs and letting the cloak stream out behind me. I'm not running away. I'm running just because it's my body and because I can. I run past vineyards, orchards, fields of wheat and then rocks and scrub. I've never been this far along the road.

Everything ahead of me is new.

Chapter Ten

In the darkness the bobbing forms of pigs glow as lake water laps around them. They glow brighter and then the spirits leave them, weaving together as they rise upwards, phosphorous tentacles reaching out for me through the night. They branch out and whisper and mew with hunger and sadness, and then I see one of these tentacles reach my slumbering form, hovering above me like a snake about to strike. It darts down, alerting the other strands. They rush at me and I open my eyes and see them, clamping my mouth shut as they try to prise open my lips. I groan and battle against them, my hands flailing uselessly at the evil all around me. I can't breathe and I'm so terrified that they've returned that I can't help but scream. As I do so, they pour inside me in their multitudes.

I wake with a jolt and hit my head hard on the rocky overhang where I fell asleep just before dawn. Black stars blur my vision and I clutch my head, thinking, *They'll be enjoying this; feeding on all this pain.* Then I remember that they're not here any more. The Master told me – maybe it was even a promise – that the spirits would never torment me again. I seem to be tormenting myself just fine without their help. I slow my breathing down and flex my hand. It doesn't try to punch me or slap me. It is my hand and under my control.

I'm thirsty, but I finished the skin of water during the night as I ran. I decide not to eat anything as it'll just make me thirstier. Hopefully I'll find a spring or well along the main road.

Judging by the sun and the heat of the day, it's past noon, so I should have the road to myself. I bundle my cloak into my satchel and head off. I pass lizards sunning themselves on the rocks and I feel relieved that I don't have to eat them. I keep looking over my shoulder to check that no one is following me. I can't shake the feeling of being watched, though, or the fear that the spirits might return. I'm already doubting the Master's words. Before, when I lived in the caves, I could never enjoy any of the food left for me because I never knew when the spirits would force me to drop it in my own faeces, or throw a particularly tasty morsel over the cliff. I feel a bit like that now; I can't really enjoy this feeling of freedom because I just don't know how long it will last. I wish I knew more about spiritual protection.

It was always my mother's great strength, knowing about spiritual protection. She always knew which gods to petition for what. When Timaeus was a plump, contented toddler, neighbours would comment loudly on his ugliness, outdoing each other with insults and giving Mother a conspiratorial wink, everyone keen to keep away the Eye. Mother knew better than all of them. We wore eye-bead bracelets as children to fool the Eye into thinking we already belonged to it; we were always careful with compliments or doing anything that might provoke jealousy in others, and Mother never left the courtyard for the forty days after each of our births, when she was most vulnerable to a barren woman's jealousy. She knew what to hang around our courtyard to protect us from spirits. She ensured that we always slept with heads covered at night to prevent spirits from whispering bad dreams to us. She knew which amulets offered best protection for travelling or during pregnancy. Protection and protecting us was always so important to her, and thinking about this makes me miss her so much. I don't know what I can do to prevent those spirits returning. Again I remind myself of the Master's words.

I know he has power and that his Father is even more powerful. "The Master's power over me," I whisper as a sort of prayer, although I don't really know who I'm praying to. I repeat this and then the memory of Mother bearing down on me with that knife comes to my mind. Even without the amulet around me, the spirits didn't leave. Her attempts at my protection were what left me tormented by those spirits in the first place. Once more I am reminded that the Master told me to go home and tell my family about the goodness of God. But which god?

These thoughts flit around my head as I walk, ignoring a growing headache from lack of water. I spot a cluster of gnarled olive trees and what looks like a roadside well. There's a tethered donkey and several slumbering forms in the dappled leaf-shade. I'm wary of people, but they're asleep and I really need to drink something, so I approach the well quietly and try to make sure the bucket doesn't clank against the sides as I lower it down.

I keep filling my skin, drinking from it and refilling it again until my belly is swollen with water. I refill it one last time and I'm about to head on when a hand clamps around my arm.

"Why the hurry?" The man has an unkempt beard, a vice-like grip and a mean sneer. He glances down at my forearm with the manacle on it, and then scans my forehead and other arm for a branding mark.

"I'm not a slave," I say.

"Then why the manacle?" He's about to wake his companions, who still seem to be fast asleep. As he turns, still gripping my arm, I swing my other one with great force at his chin. He stumbles backwards and I grab him by the hair and smash his head against the well. This knocks him out, but then the slumbering forms under the tree begin to rouse.

Manacle

I grab my satchel and water-skin and run off, water sloshing around in my stomach. I keep off the main path from then on, picking my way more slowly to either side of it, always watching for people. My knuckles really hurt where I bruised them against his chin. I don't have the power I had when *they* were in me, but I've experienced enough violence now to find that it comes quite naturally and instinctively in a way it never did before. This isn't good. It's as if I've just eaten a couple of lizards even though I'm carrying a satchel of food. Should I have reasoned more with him? Was there some other way I could have dealt with the situation? What would the Master have done? I'm really not sure. I eat some of my provisions, but half-heartedly. What if I do something worse? I don't know if I'm safe around people.

I continue and the path slopes downwards and follows the lake shoreline. As the sun sets I see ahead of me a large hill looming up from the lake-side. There's a switchback road leading up to the walled ramparts of a city straddled atop it; the City of Horses. I'm dazzled. I try to imagine what it must be like having so many people living together in one place. They can probably walk down a street and not even know some of the other people they pass. Right now that sounds quite appealing.

I pick up my pace, excited but nervous too. What will Rabba be like? What if he doesn't have work for me, or isn't interested in Tehinah's note of introduction? He could still decide that I'm a runaway, even without a brand mark. What would happen then? As I think about it, I haven't just made enemies of my village; there are all those foreign soldiers who attempted to imprison me. Somewhere out there are men with their ears bitten off, broken bones, and a commander who will never walk again, all because of me. I must get rid of this manacle.

Although it's still warm, I put on the cloak to cover my manacled wrist. As I walk closer to the hill, there are more houses, fields and vineyards, and it's impossible not to use the main road. When I pass a family, I expect the woman to clutch her children to her and for them to shrink back in fear as they see me, but they just walk straight past me, thinking nothing of it. Don't they realize that I'm a monster?

I pass a cluster of stalls selling fruit, vegetables and what smells like fish soup. I can't be trusted around people, but still I stop to ask the girl ladling the soup into bowls for directions to Rabba the tanner's. She glances down at my bare feet and I can see I will be forgotten in moments.

"Over there," she points. "Go past the dyers' street and you'll find the tanneries are all beside the lake." I follow her directions towards the shore, disappointed not to be climbing the hill to the city above. I know I'm heading in the right direction because soon I'm scuttling under dripping skeins of different coloured wool and linen. I don't want to stain the beautiful tunic the Master gave me.

It gets harder to breathe as the air grows heavy with the stench of stale urine and other equally acrid and unpleasant smells. They leave a tang at the back of my throat when I breathe through my mouth, and breathing through my nose makes my eyes water. I've entered the tanners' quarter, and now I know why it's well away from everyone else. I stop a young man and ask for Rabba's place, and he points it out to me.

"Good evening. Is Uncle Rabba at home?" I ask as politely as possible of the woman who answers my knock. She seems torn between amusement and scorn. "*Uncle* Rabba, eh?" she says. "And we are?"

I tell her the name of my village and that Tehinah sent me. Her eyes run over my fine tunic, which is at odds with my bare feet, shaven head and gaunt appearance. She goes to get Rabba. He's a short, wiry man who doesn't look much like Tehinah. He's wiping crumbs from his beard and doesn't look too happy about this interruption to his supper. I rummage in my satchel and find Tehinah's note. I'm stupid and hand it to him with my manacled hand. They both notice it and give each other a look.

Once he's finished reading it, he hands it to the woman, who looks at it helplessly and says, "What am I supposed to do with it?" Like me, I don't think she can read.

He looks up and down the street to see if there's anyone around. Then he says, "Well, you'd better come in." So I do.

The woman stands me over a grate and pours water from a stone flagon over my hands and feet. Their inner room is much larger than ours, with a doorway leading off to a second room. "Sit down, then," she says.

There's a woven reed mat with a food cloth on it and some sheepskins scattered around it. I sit down on one. "You'll be wanting food after your journey," she says, and then looks pointedly at Rabba. "And I'll be needing some help outside in the kitchen." He gets the hint and I hear them conferring in hushed whispers outside. I look around the room; in an alcove, there are some statues of gods and goddesses and a stone statue of a horse.

Rabba returns holding a steaming bowl of pork stew, which he sets before me. "We don't usually have pork at this time of year," he says, and then disappears into the kitchen again. The stew smells wonderful, and I tear up some flatbread and add it in to soak up the juices. If a boat left our village and sailed straight here, it could easily have arrived in half a day. I wonder if this is one of the pork cuts from the drowned pigs.

I try not to eat too fast, but it's a hard habit to break. I'm wiping the bowl with some bread when Rabba and the woman return. "You can have a mat for the night and a good breakfast to send you on your way tomorrow," says the woman. She seems to have taken charge.

"On my way where?"

"That's no concern of ours," she says.

"She thinks you have the look of trouble about you and we don't need trouble," says Rabba.

"Tehinah said you might have work for me with all the extra skins arriving," I say.

"And what would you know about that?" the woman asks, folding her arms.

"I was there when the herd drowned." They look at me appraisingly. "I know how large the herd was."

"We've had two boatloads of skins arrive today, and that was just our tannery. Parmenas and Timon had boats come to theirs as well," says Rabba before he's silenced by a look from the woman.

They look at each other and then the woman snaps, "Well, go on then. How large was the herd?"

"At least two thousand," I say. "Every grown pig from our village and the next was drowned. That's a lot of skins. I could help you tan them."

The woman sneers. "And what do you know about tanning?"

"I know that it's a lot of work. More work, probably, than you have the men for."

"We don't even have the money to purchase all those skins," says Rabba.

"Who does?" I counter. "I expect the villagers will take them on credit. They don't have much choice. They'll be desperate for buyers."

Rabba beams at the woman, who gives him a withering look. "You're a wily one," she says, turning back to me and narrowing her eyes as she sizes me up. "I told you he had the look of trouble about him, Rabba, didn't I?"

There's a knock at the courtyard door. "I'll watch him," she says, and Rabba goes to answer it. It's not long before he returns, breathless.

"More skins! Now come and help me get the price down. We'll have to convince them to give them to us on credit."

She shoots me one last look and then follows him.

I sit there, waiting. I can hear voices and then it's silent for a while. Then a youth comes in. He's a bit shorter and stockier than me, with lighter hair. The rims of his eyes are pink and a little inflamed. "You must be Trouble," he says with a slight smile. "Come with me." He's wearing just a waist cloth and is sun-darkened like me. I pick up my cloak and satchel. "You won't be needing those," he says. "You should leave your tunic here as well."

He scrutinizes the scars all over my torso. "The whip?" he asks as I bundle my few possessions together into the satchel. I shake my head. "It looks that way," he says with a shrug. He turns and I follow him. Behind the house and small courtyard is the main tannery. I gag.

"It's just stale piss," he laughs, as we pick our way between the shallow pits. "You look like you've seen worse."

Pass the pits is a bay, and several boats are unloading in the shallows, too heavy to beach themselves. The youth pulls off his waist cloth. "Come on," he says.

Although it's sunset and will be dark soon, I can't risk being recognized. I think for a moment and then wrap my waist cloth around my right wrist and tie it there, hiding the manacle. The men on board the boat look exhausted and barely glance up at us. We wade in almost up to our chests in the water and the first load of skins is passed to the youth, who carries them over his head. He's strong. I move forward, keeping my head down and they pass me a bundle. No one bothers to look at me properly.

Once the skins have been unloaded, a fisherman calls us over. "You'll need two of you with this," he says as he and another fisherman haul a quivering, dripping sack over to us. It's too heavy to carry, so we let it sink and then drag it to shore.

"Brains," says the youth, and looks at me as if I'm stupid. "For softening the skins."

We deal with two more sacks and then the boat leaves. We then start unloading the contents of the second boat and by the time we move on to the third boat it's almost dark and my muscles ache.

The youth wades forward to the third boat to collect the first bundle of skins. "Have you got it?" the fisherman asks, and I almost cry out. It's Timaeus. I move forward with my head down and Tim passes me a bundle of skins. We're so close and I'm desperate to get a proper look at him in the fading light, but I mustn't give myself away.

"I just need a moment to catch my breath," I say as we reach the bay. The youth swears and goes back without me. I watch as Timaeus places another load of skins on him. Tim's as tall as me now and the hard work and a good diet of fish have filled him out and corded his back and arms with muscle. It makes him look older than me, as I'm so scrawny. He even has the beginnings of a beard. His face has lost its softness and is angular but not unkind. I want to dash into the water, throw my arms around him and plead with him that we forget everything that has come between us.

"Come on," says the youth, and I trail behind him to collect the last loads. I glance up quickly, scanning for Rufus and his crewmates, but they're not there. This isn't their boat. Timaeus must be helping others, just as Mother said he would. I wonder if he's been blamed yet for what happened; paying for his brother yet again. They're all too tired to notice me, and I let my hand briefly brush Tim's arm as I collect the last bundle of skins. The sail is already lowered and the boat pulling away by the time I reach the shore, and once I drop this last bundle, I unwrap my waist cloth from my wrist and use it to wipe tears from my eyes.

"You'll get used to it," says the youth. "It's the stale piss. It makes your eyes water." He puts his waist cloth back on, so I do the same with mine. "It'll be a long night," he says. "Every skin's got to be put in a pit."

The woman who calls me Trouble comes to the pits with several pitch torches. She sets them up and then comes back with one of them alight and uses it to light the others. There's a harvest moon, too, which helps.

In the flickering light I notice a narrow aqueduct providing the pits with water which can be channelled into any one of them or allowed to flow straight into the lake. First we weigh the skins down with rocks and then fill each pit with water.

We drag a sack of brains up to the nearest pit which is full of water and cut the sack open, spilling its contents into the water. I retch at the smell.

"Once the skins have been soaked and scraped, we'll put them in here to soften them," explains the youth. I still don't know his name. There's no sign of Rabba or the woman. They're probably asleep by now. We work through the night and by the time we've finished emptying the last sack, the moon is already setting. We trudge down to the lake one last time and wash ourselves.

"What's your name?" I ask the youth as we head back to the tannery.

"Nicanor," he says.

"Are you Rabba's son?"

He gives a mirthless laugh that answers that question but leaves me with more.

"I'm Phineas, or just Phin," I say. I don't think he was ever going to ask.

He leads me into the courtyard to a small room beside a vine. Inside, I can just make out a rolled-up sleeping mat and blanket, which Nicanor unrolls. "You sleep here," he says, pointing to a sleeping mat beside it. My cloak, tunic and satchel are piled on top of it. I roll out the mat, crawl under the blanket and don't even remember falling asleep.

"Come on, up, up!" says a sharp woman's voice. I'm groggy and don't feel as if I've slept much. For a moment I have no idea where I am. Nicanor swears softly. "Come on. If you're quick, you can have a bite to eat before you start unloading."

I sit up, breathe deeply and then wish I hadn't. I wonder if I'll ever get used to the smell. Nicanor rouses himself and outside we find a food cloth and a flat basket of bread, dates, cucumbers, olives and some fried lumps of pork. We eat quickly, still in just our waist cloths, and then head down to the bay. Several more heavily laden boats have arrived. Now that it's daylight I'm more worried about being recognized.

"If you bring the skins to shore, I'll carry them up here to the pits," I say. Nicanor thinks for a moment. It's not a great idea as it means the boats will have to wait longer, but he'd much rather be immersed in the cool of the water, so he nods.

We work like this until it's time to unload sacks. These require both of us, so I wind my waist cloth around the manacle again and join Nicanor beside the boat. I look up and see Rufus in one of the boats. He looks right at me. I take care to stay as submerged as possible so my scars aren't obvious and just stare through him as if he were a stranger. This seems to work. No one has really seen what I look like for two years under all that dirt and matted hair. I don't even know how much my own face has changed. Anyway, they have more important things to worry about and wouldn't expect to find me here.

There are five fishing boats in our village and over the course of the day, all five of them arrive at tanners' bay. Even this is not enough to ferry the skins, so other boats commissioned from elsewhere also arrive. One or two other tanners nod at Nicanor and appraise me briefly before getting back to their work. I spot Timaeus in one of the boats. I'm both relieved and disappointed when it steers in towards one of the other tanneries.

The woman – is she Rabba's wife? – walks down towards the bay with a skin of water and some pastries filled with greens. I blush and quickly tie on my waist cloth. "You're a tanner now," says Nicanor, rolling his eyes. "There's no time for any of that."

She offers the pastries to us without ceremony.

"How many more boats are there?" she yells at one of the fishermen unloading for our neighbouring tanner.

"Six or seven," he shouts back.

"You should be finished by sundown," she tells us, and heads off.

"Is that Rabba's wife?" I ask, just to be sure.

Nicanor nods. "Demarchia," he says.

By the time we've got the bundles of skins submerged in the water pits and poured the sacks of brains into the growing pool of brain slurry, the next boats are waiting. My body is used to the sun, but my naked scalp is burning. Wading deep into the lake is the best part of the day. We are both exhausted by the time the last boat is unloaded and once we've finished, we slope off to the lake, submerging our aching backs and shoulders beneath the waters.

I'd expected Nicanor to have a little curiosity about me, or at least attempt a few questions, but he doesn't, and I like him more as a result.

"Want to swim?" he says.

"I never learned," I say.

"It's not hard."

Whether it's exhaustion or the manacle, which is heavy, or whether I'm just not very good, I'm struggling to copy him, and eventually he sighs in exasperation and then disappears under the water. Back on shore we stand in the evening breeze to dry off and then head back to Rabba's. My stomach grumbles in anticipation.

We're given supper outside under the vine. More pork stew and my second hot meal in two years.

"Every pit full," says Rabba, appearing and looking as pleased with himself as if he'd actually done some work. "So, how was Trouble, then?" he asks Nicanor, who just shrugs. "Tomorrow you can change the water in the storage pits and move the first skins into the piss pits."

"Both of us?" I ask.

"Yes, yes," Rabba says dismissively. It seems I'm allowed to stay. I wonder if I should ask about a contract or wages, but I sense it might be better to simply accept that for now I have a roof over my head and food in my belly.

"Rabba, I'm doing calculations," shouts Demarchia from inside, and Rabba rolls his eyes but goes and joins her.

I sit there in silence with Nicanor. After all these hours of working together, although I'm not a great talker I find myself asking, "So, how long have you been a tanner?"

He stares back at me. "Why is there a manacle around your wrist?"

"It's a long story. Do you really want to know?"

Nicanor shrugs. We sit there in silence for a while. Timaeus used to be the only person I could just sit with in silence and for that to be all right. Nicanor picks meditatively at meat between his teeth and then gets up, takes a lamp from our room and lights it from the kitchen embers. I follow him into our room and he places the lamp in the wall alcove before a statue of a horse. He whispers a few prayers to it and then unrolls his mat and bedding and is soon breathing deeply.

I sit there staring at the lamplight. Who should I pray to? I don't know anything about this horse and I can't remember much about the different gods and goddesses, except that none of them helped me when I really needed them. I wonder which gods the Master prays to. I'm not sure if what I'm doing is praying, or even who I'm praying to, but as I look at the lamplight I whisper, "Thank you that the spirits are gone. Thank you that the Master came and freed me. Thank you that his Father has a plan for me." It feels nice just talking and not having to hide who I am, or worrying about what the response will be. I still wonder how I'm to walk this road the Master talked about, and what it all means. Maybe I'll think more about it when I'm not so tired. I lean over, blow out the lamp and fall quickly to sleep.

Chapter Eleven

The spirits force themselves inside me, prising my lips and then my teeth open. They swarm over me like wild bees and I feel a crushing sense of despair.

"Get out, get out!" I shriek, and then I hear choking. I wake. The choking continues. It's Nicanor. I'm clutching his throat. I let go of him quickly and he rains down curses on me.

"I'm so sorry," I say, still panting, my body drenched in sweat.

"If you ever do something like that again…" he says.

Nicanor is sullen over breakfast, but once we're in the pits he explains the importance of keeping the water in the storage pits fresh and his mood brightens. He's a natural teacher, even though I don't think he realizes it. We're interrupted by Rabba, who tells us that the piss pots have arrived. I expect to see rows of small urine-filled pots but instead there's a train of donkeys heavy with bulging pigskins strapped on each side. We lead the donkeys to the piss pit and haul the first pigskin off, undo the neck and pour an acrid yellow stream into it.

"We'll top this pit up with water and pour the rest of the piss into a second pit. Whenever you need a piss, make sure you do it in here," says Nicanor. "We need all the piss we can get. With all these pigskins there might even be a shortage."

"Where does it come from?"

"There are pots outside every tavern, the market, the crossroads. He collects it and sells it to the tanners," says Nicanor, pointing at the old man holding the tether to the train of donkeys. He clearly has no desire to help with this decanting.

Once the skins are all empty and the old man has left with his donkeys, Nicanor adds water to both pits and then we drag our first batch of pigskins over to them.

"We'll need to weigh the skins down so they don't float," says Nicanor, pulling off his waist cloth and wading into the nearest pit, a large stone in one hand and some skins in the other. I'm still standing by the side. I can't believe he's wading around in other people's piss. He turns to me impatiently and curses.

So I take off my waist cloth and wade in after him. The urine stings small cuts and grazes I didn't realize I had. We submerge each skin and pinion it in place with heavy stones. My eyes are streaming by this point, but I can't wipe them with my piss-drenched hands. Once we've finished doing this, we have to drag out skins from the old piss pit, which smells even worse, and pile them into a cleaning pit with running water from the aqueduct flowing through it. We then repeat the whole process with more skins which we submerge in the old piss pit. I keep trying to breathe through my mouth, not wipe my eyes and control an overwhelming desire to retch, not least because every time I do, Nicanor curses me for my softness.

"We'll start scouring the old skins after lunch," he says finally. He picks up an inner-gourd from a small niche beside one of the pits and trots down towards the lake. I follow him and we take it in turns to use the gourd to scrub our arms and legs.

We eat lunch under the vine and after being knee-deep in a pit of stale urine, the courtyard doesn't seem to smell at all. After lunch, Nicanor leads me out beside the pits to an open place screened by trees and shaded by another vine. The ground beneath is flat and hard. He hands me a blunt, broken sword blade.

"No one else wants them and they make great tools. Why pay for something you can get for free?" he says.

We tug one of the old skins from under a rock in the pit with running water and drag it over to the open space, placing it in the shade of the vine. Nicanor kneels on it and starts the scraping and scouring process, using the dull edge of the sword to lift off any dead bits of flesh or skin. Chickens lurk nearby, scratching in the dust, and every now and then Nicanor collects the dead bits of skin and flings them in their direction. The chickens have clearly been waiting for this and attack in a flurry of pecking.

The scoured skin goes back under flowing water and we work together on the next one. This process is laborious. I can't imagine how many months it would have taken Nicanor to deal with all the skins we've unloaded if he was working alone. As it is, I feel reassured that they'll need me for the rest of the summer at the very least.

At first, the best thing about this hard work is that it doesn't give me time to think or to worry. I'm just a tanner boy working on a skin. But then I look up and see the row of pomegranate trees with their blood-coloured fruits still small. Why did they have to be pomegranate trees? I look down where I kneel and for a moment the blunt blade in my hands isn't scraping a skin, it's scraping the blood, splinters of skull and brain matter from Aqub's head over our courtyard. I shake my head to get rid of the vision and try not to think of anything except the animal skin in front of me. My plan sort of works, but still I think about the blood that pooled around me. I am a murderer and I shouldn't be here scraping skins. I should have been executed. If Nicanor knew the things these hands have done, he would know that I'm monstrous. I can't shake this feeling and fall asleep that night feeling fraudulent. I'm free, but I'm not, because what I did has not been undone. It never can be.

The following morning I'm woken by Nicanor. I claw at him and growl. He learns to keep out of my grasp when he shakes me from the nightmares. My dreams seem to be the one part of my body I can't control and they always take me back to the caves. Once I'm awake, I start each morning as if it was my first, with a palpable sense of relief, even when I have to wade into the stinking slurry of piss or pig brains to weigh down skins with a heavy stone or drag them out. But there's usually something that reminds me of what I really am. That I'm not the young tanner. That however much my hands become raw from the stale piss and the scouring, they will always have blood on them.

Rabba and Demarchia still call me Trouble, which makes me appreciate Nicanor more, for calling me nothing. Although he never speaks when a shrug will do, he's a patient teacher and eventually I learn to swim with him in the evenings. If we race, he always beats me, but then we run along the shoreline to dry off and it's my turn to come first. Gradually my ribs don't stick out so much, my most recent cuts begin to fade a little. I fill out and gain muscle and my hair grows again.

There are only three people in my life now – four if you include the old man who delivers the piss. The boys from the other tanneries keep a pretty similar schedule to us and we see them swimming in the lake at the end of the day but we never talk to them, and simply nod to each other. It's probably best that way. I still don't trust myself around people and I wonder what the other tanner boys think of my manacle. I'm glad that most visitors to the tanneries come only for business and hope that any speculation about me – if there is any – remains here on tanners' bay.

As my hair begins to curl again, I ask Demarchia if she has a mirror I can borrow.

"I wouldn't start preening," she says mockingly. "The girls

will smell you coming long before they can see you. You're a tanner now." Still, she fetches me a spotted brass mirror which needs a polish. I don't really know what I look like any more. As I examine myself I see how patchy my beard is, probably from when I used to pull it out when they were still in me. I decide to try to shave it regularly. The scratch marks where I raked my fingernails across my cheeks have gone completely, which is a relief. I have a strong jaw, straight teeth and a good nose, and decide I look quite good.

"That's enough for one day," says Demarchia, as if she can read my mind, and snatches the mirror back.

"I'd like to shave my beard," I say. "I don't have a razor or anything. We've never talked about my wages."

"Hmpf," she says. "No good ever comes of young men and mirrors. Next you'll be wanting money to fritter away in taverns and brothels."

She says no more on the matter, but she's clearly talked with her husband about it because that evening Rabba asks us for a report on the number of scoured skins soaking in the brain slurry that just need a final washing and oiling.

"We should have twenty skins ready for market by the end of the week," says Nicanor.

"Good," says Rabba. "Get them ready on time and I'll take you with me into the city. Let's get them sold before the whole market is flooded with pigskins. Don't worry, you'll get your cut."

"What about this?" I say, and lift up my wrist with the manacle.

"You'll just have to keep it covered," says Rabba.

Three days later, we wait outside the tannery with several stacks of skins while Rabba haggles with a donkey owner over the cost to take us to market.

Once we get going, I walk ahead with Nicanor and ask him how much our cut is. He just shrugs. "You must have some idea," I say.

"He cheats other people where he can, but he doesn't cheat us. We're family."

I hope he's right. I have plans for my money. I've wrapped the prayer shawl Tehinah gave me around my wrist. It looks a bit odd but I don't know how else to disguise it. The path starts zigzagging up the steep hillside but we don't slow down and I enjoy being a little out of breath, taking great lungfuls of sweet, untainted air. I sniff the tunic which the Master gave me, wondering if I carry with me the stench of the tannery. If I do, I can't tell. The sun is just rising and there are other traders on the road with donkey trains and even a caravan of camels. We plod through the main city gate and I can't help craning my neck around, taking in the massive ramparts and walls. There are rotting skulls stuck on spikes. I point them out to Nicanor, who simply rolls his eyes.

"They're just criminals. Stop pointing and gawping like some village boy," he says. The thing is, I am a village boy, but I try not to look quite so awestruck by everything. It's hard not to look upwards. Only a few houses in my village have upper rooms but here the buildings seem to go up to the sky, with some as many as three or four storeys. The city teems with people; more than I've ever seen in my life. There are foreign soldiers in uniform, men wearing just waist cloths who must be slaves, merchants in tunics, priests in robes, perfumed women dripping in jewellery and surrounded by serving girls. I have to make myself stop staring at the darkest man I've ever seen, with hair so curly it looks like black fur. We pass a group of bejewelled women with braided hair and heavy make-up who call out to us. "I'll be seeing you later," Nicanor calls back as we pass them.

We pass several temples. I'm curious about what goes on inside, even if the gods have brought me nothing but trouble. I wish my mother was here and could make her offerings.

The market is big enough to be divided into sections and we head towards the sound of hammering, passing the potters, the coppersmiths and blacksmiths and then the carpenters until we arrive at the leatherworkers' section. The skins are unloaded and Rabba chooses one that he deems the softest and supplest and starts visiting the different workshops with it. He's gone for what seems like forever, but I don't mind because Nicanor lets me wander into a workshop that produces saddlery, whips and reins. The workshop next door focuses on wine-skins and water-skins and then there are several workshops producing every conceivable form of sandal.

Eventually Rabba emerges from a workshop making water-skins with a man in a leather apron. Rabba looks sullen as the man browses through the skins drawing attention to defects, real or imaginary. Haggling ensues. Rabba curses, cries out in pain, laughs hysterically and calls on the gods for justice. Finally coins are counted into a pouch and we are told by a scowling Rabba to carry the skins into the workshop.

"Being robbed is thirsty work, boys," he says loudly as we make to leave. "Come on, let's find a tavern."

It's only after we're out of earshot that he cackles and crows about the price he got. We find a nearby place, which is just a few benches in the shade of some woven reed matting. Rabba buys us a skin of wine and doesn't complain when I do no more than sip mine. I've seen what wine can do. He lifts his clay cup and makes a toast. "To Trouble and his many pigs," he says, cackling again as he and Nicanor down their cups. Then he reaches into his pouch and draws out a handful of coins for us each.

"Nicanor gets extra for teaching you," he says, which seems fair enough.

They finish the wine-skin. "So," says Rabba, belching and then patting Nicanor affectionately, "are we ready? It's time the girls of our city had a little Trouble."

They both grin at me and then I realize what they mean. "I'll be back at the tannery before sunset," I say, smiling sheepishly. "There's something I need to do."

"Such as?" says Rabba, curious. But Nicanor just shrugs and is already sauntering back towards the girls we saw earlier. Rabba goes trotting after him, calling, "Leave some for me."

Once they're gone I look at the coins in my hand, trying to calculate their total value in my head. I'm hoping there'll be enough left over to buy some sandals, but first I head to the blacksmiths' section of the market. I feign interest in horseshoes and nails, browsing until I round a corner and reach the workshop furthest from the main thoroughfare and as private as I'm going to find. A lone smith works at the anvil. He's an old, wiry man with burn marks up and down his forearms. After a while he senses me watching him and looks up from his hammering.

"I'll wait until you're done with that," I say. I'm not sure where to start.

He grunts and continues with his work, the horseshoe hissing when it is plunged into water. "So?" he says, looking up and wiping his hands on a leather apron.

"I was just looking at the burns on your arms," I say. I can tell he's wondering why I'm wasting his time. "I have scars from where I used to cut myself. I spent two years trying to kill myself." I open the neck of my tunic for him to see.

"So, you want to lay your head on my anvil and have me finish the job for you, eh?" There's mirth in his voice.

"I had spirits living inside me, controlling my body. I was trapped like a prisoner. Death would have been better. I lost my family, and the girl I loved. The spirits were more powerful than me, but also more powerful than anyone else. With them in me, I destroyed a whole section of soldiers more than once. I hurt a lot of people." I unwind the prayer shawl from around my right wrist. "The spirits broke the other manacle and the chain between them. Here, feel it. You know I couldn't have done that. They must have left this one to remind me that I would always be their slave."

The blacksmith examines the manacle and then takes my

other arm. He can see the chafing scars but there is no brand mark. "Do you know what the punishment for freeing slaves is?" he asks.

"You can see I'm not a slave. I've never been branded," I say. "And anyway, who would put such a large manacle on a slave?"

This causes him to ponder. He examines it more closely, and I can see he's thinking of the best way to remove it. "Taking this off is easy. Doing it without you losing your hand will be the challenge," he says.

I hold out my other palm. "This is all I have," I say.

He doesn't look at the coins. "I'm bored with horseshoes," he says, and almost smiles.

He tries pincers but the band is too thick, then he tries heating the metal but that's not possible without it burning my wrist. Eventually he sends a boy to fetch ice. There are stores of it, collected in winter from the heights nearby and kept cool underground in cellars.

While we're waiting for the ice, I tell him about the Master and how he had the power to banish the spirits from me. He asks me who the Master's gods are but I don't really know. Then I remember something. "He told me to tell everyone about what he's done for me and about the goodness of God. But I don't know which god he meant."

"They only have one on the north shore," says the blacksmith. "He must be the one who helped you." I think he's right.

The smithy puts me to work on the bellows and begins to heat up a strip of metal until it's glowing white and then becomes liquid. Once the ice arrives he alternates between pouring molten metal over the manacle where it was sealed together before, and then plunging my arm into an ice bath before the manacle burns me. This, he explains between hammer blows, should weaken the metal and make it easier to break. I'm worried it'll buckle or bend, trapping my wrist and cutting off the blood supply. We repeat this process until eventually the hammer makes a crack in

Chris Aslan

the metal. A few more carefully aimed blows and it splits open, wide enough for me to wriggle my wrist out.

I grin as my arm seems to want to float in the air. There are a few fresh burn marks on my wrist and it bleeds a little, but on the whole I've come out remarkably unscathed. At last I feel free.

I then haggle with the blacksmith. He doesn't want to take payment, but I insist and eventually he takes my coins. I'm still not sure if they're enough. "Where can I find out more about the god of the north shore?" I ask him, just before I leave.

"If you want to find out anything, go to the baths," he says, and drops a few coins back into my hand. "They aren't free."

I find one of the city bathhouses and I'm about to go in, but then decide to wait until next time. Instead, I buy a second waist cloth. I'll save it for when I'm not working at the tannery. I should probably be saving money for the future, but that would require thinking about my future, which I'm not ready to do just yet.

I make it back to Rabba's before sunset. Demarchia seems surprised to see me.

"Back so early? Perhaps I misnamed you," she says.

I eat alone and Nicanor is still not back by the time I prepare for sleep. I've lit the lamp and placed it in the alcove, and as I stare at its light I pray to the God-of-the-North-Shore. I don't know what his real name is, but I thank him for the blacksmith and that now I'm truly free.

I'm not, though. The next morning, I still find myself clawing at Nicanor as he attempts to wake me, and I'm bathed in sweat and panting with fear.

Chapter Twelve

Life takes on a monotonous rhythm, but one thing I like about spending most of every day working is that it doesn't leave much time for thinking. I have to work at not thinking, though. I've taken to scraping and scouring with my back to the pomegranate trees with their ripening fruit now the colour of blood that's about to congeal. I still wake from nightmares every morning. I try reminding myself of the Master's promise that the spirits will never be allowed to torment me again, but I feel empty. I want my life to be full of something else. What would be the opposite of spirits? That's what I want. It feels like an itch that I can never reach because it's inside me. Again, I try not to think about it but it's always there.

Nicanor never asked me what happened to the manacle. A local butcher brings us sheep, goat and cow skins which we also tan. We're still mainly working our way through the pigskins, though. We boys do all the work, Rabba does the deals and Demarchia keeps us all in order. She still calls me Trouble, but says it with more affection now. She and Rabba seem happy with my work and don't push me to talk about myself. It occurs to me that the blacksmith – a virtual stranger – knows more about me than Nicanor does.

I vaguely keep track of the days and weeks, mainly by the waxing and waning of the moon. Soon there are enough skins for us to join Rabba on another trip up into the city. We reach the main road when Rabba whispers to us, "Keep your eyes on the road." From his tone I can hear something is wrong and glance up to see what's ahead. There are people milling around, including a number of foreign soldiers, and tall posts have been hammered vertically into the ground at the crossroads where the road up the hill to the city begins. Each post has a cross-beam and hanging, nailed, are naked and bloodied men contorting weakly.

I gasp and Nicanor puts a hand on my shoulder, squeezing too tight. I know it means I'm to shut up and say nothing. As we come closer we can hear the weeping of women and the moans of the nailed. I look – I can't help myself. There are five posts. One of the condemned is unconscious – maybe dead, I don't know. The others, though, they use the large nails that have been hammered through their feet to push themselves up to breathe, gasping and then collapsing. They keep repeating the process and it looks horrific. My mouth fills with bile.

"Mercy, the sword," I hear one of them whimper. I want to run, I want to be sick, and I want to help them – whatever it is they've supposedly done. I don't do any of these things. We pass them and a sign chalked on a large piece of slate. I don't know what it says.

Only when we're halfway up the road towards the city do we breathe easily again. "I've never seen a nailing before," I say quietly to Nicanor. "What did they do?"

Nicanor sighs impatiently. "What does it matter? It's nothing to do with us." I can see it bothered him too. I look over to Rabba, who avoids my gaze and walks on more purposefully than before.

I don't get the chance to dwell on this for long, as soon we're in the market and I get to see more leatherwork as Rabba haggles over prices. I watch over the shoulder of someone stamping motifs into cut pieces of leather, wishing I could learn to do something that skilful, aware that I'm just a tanner and that I probably smell.

Once the deal has been struck, Rabba takes us for a drink in the tavern and hands us each our wages. This time I'm given the same amount as Nicanor. I ask Rabba how much a good pair of sandals costs, and the price of a shaving kit and admission to the public baths. He warns me of pickpockets, so I leave the rest of my coins with him for safe-keeping.

"Is the lake not good enough for you?" says Nicanor.

"I'm sick of this patchy beard. It needs to come off," I say. "I don't mind being a tanner, but I don't want to always smell like one."

"And I don't mind being a married man. I just don't want to always act like one," says Rabba with a wink to Nicanor. We leave the tavern and they head for the girls while I make my way back to the leather section of the market and haggle over a pair of nondescript but well-made sandals, managing to get them for the price Rabba said. I should be pleased with my wages and my new sandals as I make my way to the baths, but I can't shake the image of those poor, nailed men.

There are stalls outside the baths selling bathing kits of razors, scrapers, and oil. I make my purchase, pay the entrance fee and walk through the door for free men into the changing room. Mindful of what Nicanor said the first time I entered the city, I try not to stare at the frescoes on the wall or the opulent marble archways. I take off my clothes and hand them to an attendant who looks me up and down. I'm so used to my scars that I tend to forget about them. I can see him searching for a brand mark.

"You won't find one," I say. "I'm not a slave or a criminal." I take my bathing kit and follow others through a wooden door into the first room of the baths. Steam rises, and condensation trickles down the walls just like the sweat running down our bodies. I can feel my scalp prickle as the sweat begins to flow. I copy others around me, finding an empty place on the marble, then almost jumping up again after sitting down, as the stone itself is heated. It's too hot to talk, and too steamy for anyone to make out my scars. I decide that this is my favourite room, even though I haven't been to the others yet. When I feel faint I move to the next room, which is a little cooler, and I oil myself and then start scraping the dirt off me. There are polished brass mirrors on the wall and I go over to one and shave off my beard.

Finally, having briefly swum in the cold pool of the last room, I emerge into the courtyard to dry in the air. Young men throw the discus, race each other and practise gymnastics and wrestling. In the shade of trees are knots of older men, gossiping.

This part of the baths serves a purely social function and lacks the bustle of the market. If I'm ever to find someone who knows about the man from the north shore, it'll be here. I scan the courtyard. I wonder if I should look to see who is circumcised, but other than it being some kind of mutilation, I don't really know what it is. I offer up a quick prayer to the God-of-the-North-Shore.

"Hey, the arena isn't for slaves," says someone behind me. I turn and face a paunchy middle-aged man.

"I'm not a slave," I say, and let him scrutinize me for a brand mark.

"How do you explain all this, then?" says the man, pointing at my scars. "Was it the lash? Are you a criminal?"

A few others gather around us. Then the words of the Master come to me. He told me to go throughout the region of the ten towns and tell others about what he'd done for me. This is one of the ten towns. Now I know what to do.

"Look at the pattern of the scars," I say, raising my voice a little. "You can see they're not from a lash or a whip. I did this to myself. I cut myself with rocks. It was all they would let me do. I wasn't allowed to kill myself, even though I tried many times." The man with a paunch says nothing but he seems interested, and a younger man passing by us stops to listen too. "For two years I was plagued with spirits. Every day they tormented me. I was a prisoner in my own body."

I tell my story and more people gather. I'm not a great talker and I've never spoken to a large group like this before, but somehow the words seem to come. I explain about the power the spirits gave me and the attempts made to imprison me.

As I'm speaking, almost out of my field of vision, one of the wrestlers strides purposefully towards the crowd, glistening with oil. He gets closer but doesn't stop, and the next thing I know, he's punched me hard on my jaw, knocking me to the ground.

"Keep back," says the man to the crowd as I rub my jaw and try to sit up. It's already starting to swell. The man is wide-eyed and fearful. I feel dizzy and I'm trying to understand why he just hit me, and then suddenly it makes sense.

"Were you one of the soldiers?" I ask.

"He's dangerous," says the man, and I notice his foreign accent now and his lighter-coloured hair.

"How badly did I hurt you?" I ask. The crowd seem confused because he's the one who just punched me.

"I just got a broken rib," says the man. He narrows his eyes and looks closer. "It was you, wasn't it?"

"It was this body," I say, "but it wasn't me. You know that. How could I have overpowered you and all the others? Look at me. I'm the one on the floor."

He comes over and helps me to my feet, brushing ineffectually at dirt that has stuck to my oiled skin. He looks me over. "You've filled out a bit and cleaned up, but it was definitely you," he says. Then he grabs my wrist and I wonder if he's going to wrestle me to the ground or hit me again. Instead, he lifts my arm in the air and calls his friends over. "Hey, Felix, Demetrius, over here," he shouts. By now everyone is coming over. Who doesn't like a good fight? "Come and meet the victor!" He puts a friendly arm around me. My jaw really hurts. "Last time I saw this one, he was living like an animal in a cave, all wild and half-starved. We couldn't figure out why they'd plied us with wine and then begged us to arrest him, this skinny little boy. Why couldn't they do it themselves? We had no idea what we were walking into. Next thing we know he opens his mouth and all these different voices speak back at us, warning us to keep away. Then he attacks us, outnumbered ten to one. All hell breaks loose." He takes great pleasure in describing each grisly detail of violence and the crowd enjoy listening. "I've never lost a fight to anyone, have I, Felix?" he says. "But this skinny little kid destroyed our entire section." He turns to me. "So, what happened? How did you end up... you know... you again?"

My jaw hurts when I talk, but I've known worse. I start to tell them about the Master's arrival and his power over the spirits, and then about the pigs. It seems that everyone's heard about what happened with the pigs. "So," I say, "I came to the baths today because I was hoping you could help me. Do any of you know about this man? All I know is that he's from the north shore."

"I know who he is," says a man with short, curly, copper-coloured hair, speaking with a foreign accent. "My commander had a servant who was like a son to him. The boy was dying and our commander went and found him – this holy man you're talking about – and begged him to help. The holy man didn't even see the boy. He just said that he would be well, and then he was."

Someone else talks about a friend of their cousin who saw this same man cure an old hunchback and someone else talks of lepers being cured. Then speculation breaks out among the older men over whether the man is one of the gods come down in human form. It turns out that several of the crowd are priests from different temples and they start hotly debating which of the gods it might be.

The soldier puts an arm around me and steers me back into the baths. "Come on, let's get you cleaned up," he says cheerfully. We enter the pool and his smile fades. "Listen," he whispers to me, "I got a broken rib but now I'm fine. No hard feelings. But that's me. From what I've heard, you've done a lot worse to others. Don't think they'll forget, either. If they ever see you again, they'll kill you. Stop telling people who you are if you don't want to end up nailed." We clamber out of the pool. "Go," he whispers, and I take his advice.

My new sandals chafe as I hurry back down the hill. At the bottom, the men still hang from their posts. Another one seems to be dead or unconscious, but it's not the one who was crying out for mercy. He and two others still moan and pant as they fight for every breath. One of them weeps and begs for water.

"Hey, you," calls out one of the soldiers and I freeze, feeling my insides turn to liquid. "Give the man a drink."

I turn and see some soldiers squatting in the shade of a nearby tree, playing dice. There's a pole with a sponge propped next to a water jar. I dip the sponge and pass it up to the man who is moaning for water. He sucks at it greedily and I have to dip it in the water twice more and pass it up, trying not to let the pole shake from my trembling hands. I pass it up a fourth time but he's too exhausted for more and concentrates instead on levering himself up on the nail in his feet to snatch another breath.

The soldiers are back at their dice and I put the pole and sponge back, keeping my eyes to the ground, and continue on. My heart is pounding and as soon as I turn the corner I piss against the nearest tree. All I can think is that this could have been me. The soldier in the baths was right. I have made some serious enemies and now there are no spirits inside to protect me. If those soldiers came for me, I would be powerless to resist them. And now I've seen what they can do. That could have been me nailed at the crossroads. I've known suffering, but nothing like that.

I'm not really free at all. Some bonds can be broken, but even though I've not got a manacle around my wrist, I'll always be bound to the things I've done. Maybe I'll never truly be free.

When I arrive back at the tannery, Demarchia asks me why I'm so pale and I mention the nailings. "It's their second day up there," she says grimly. "They're strong young men, those insurgents, and some of them will still be up there and alive tomorrow." I leave before she notices my swollen jaw. I go straight to my room, taking my new sandals off and leaving them at the door. My feet are raw from the straps, and they hurt. I imagine how much worse it would be to have a long rusty nail hammered through them. I go to bed without praying and without supper. How can I have let myself get so careless?

About a week later, I'm sitting with Nicanor over supper under the vine, and he says, "I hear you were asking about that man from the north shore." How does he know about this? I never see Nicanor talking to anyone. I glance up and Nicanor is looking at me with expectation.

"Yes, I'm interested in him," I say.

"He gives his followers food," says Nicanor, gnawing on a bone. "That's what people talk about up on the hill."

"Why would people talk about that?"

"He takes one person's lunch and makes it enough to feed everyone there. They even take food home with them."

"But that's impossible."

"Exactly." Nicanor grins and belches.

"What else have you heard?" I say, and he sighs.

"I don't know. Talk to Hanan."

"Who?"

"He's a cock-cutter up on the hill. Won't work with pigskins because it's against their law. I'd fire him if it was up to me, but everyone knows he's one of the best leatherworkers in the market."

I nod and Nicanor goes back to his bone. I still can't figure out how he knows so many people when he never seems to speak to anyone.

The evenings get cooler although it's still warm during the day. It's the season of pomegranates and apples. We've worked about a third of the pigskins by now. They seem to get easier to scrape, which I assume is just me getting better at my job until Nicanor explains that the longer soaking time makes the skins easier to work.

We make another trip up the hill. I think about making excuses not to go, worried about being recognized by one of the soldiers. It's not likely, given how much my appearance has changed, but after seeing those nailings, I don't want to take the risk. Then I remember what Nicanor said about Hanan the leatherworker. I want to find out more about the Master, so I decide to risk it and go.

I needn't have worried; we've barely arrived before Rabba storms out of the last workshop fuming, and beckons us to follow him back to the tannery with the donkeys still carrying all our skins. It turns out that the glut of pigskins means the price has dropped drastically as the leatherworkers can't keep pace with us. Plus, now that the weather is cooling off, villagers are slaughtering their pigs for meat, so that's even more skins on the market.

Back home, Rabba and Demarchia confer and decide to store skins to sell later as we've made good profits in recent months and Demarchia has enough to run the household for some time before we'd need to make another sale. I'm disappointed not to track down Hanan, but then I remember the soldier's words and decide that it's probably a good thing for me to lay low. Does this make me a fugitive? Will I always be watching over my shoulder?

Again, I try not to think about the future, but I don't know how long I can keep putting this off.

When the autumn storms hit the lake, I feel the old wildness stirring in me, like when the spirits were still there. Me and Nicanor love swimming in the lake when the waves are high, although we make sure to keep close to shore. The days shorten and soon we stop swimming altogether and only use the lake for washing swiftly, emerging with chattering teeth. Rabba gives us tatty old tunics to wear while we work the skins as it's too cold now to work them in just waist cloths.

I've taken to praying every night, usually after Nicanor has gone to sleep, which never takes long. I pray to the God of the Master, and just tell him what I'm thinking and what's happened that day. Sometimes it really makes me miss Timaeus, because he was the one I used to talk to like this. I still feel empty. It's not that I would ever want the spirits back, but I wish there was something good that I could be filled up with instead.

The nightmares continue to plague me. Nicanor is used to them now and I never wake choking him again, as he knows how to keep out of my reach in those frenzied moments of waking. I wonder if I'll ever be totally free of the spirits, or if they'll always inhabit my nights. I realize that all my life I've been afraid of something. First it was the Evil Eye and the spirits my mother warned me about, and then it was Aqub. I remember how I would tense whenever he was around, and the cruel things he did to me. Some of those things are too shameful for me to ever mention to anyone. Then the spirits took me over and I wasn't afraid of Aqub or even a whole army of soldiers. But I was afraid of the spirits and afraid that they would never leave me or let me die. Now, I'm afraid of the spirits coming back, even though the Master promised that they wouldn't, and I'm afraid of being found and punished by the foreign soldiers, even though the Master told me to tell people about what he's done for me. Maybe it's fear that's kept me alive so far, but I'm tired of always being on my guard; always looking over my shoulder.

Our household marks religious holidays that revolve around various gods. One day we're kept back from the pits to help Demarchia prepare a feast for the other tannery owners. They all offer gifts to the gods who have blessed us with so many pigskins this year. Rabba goes up to the leatherworkers on the hill alone, taking just one skin with him, wanting to test the current market. He returns that evening looking grim and begins conferring with Demarchia in front of us.

The price for pigskins has sunk even further, and it's unlikely to have picked up by spring, which is how long we can afford to wait without making a sale. "We need to start repaying Tehinah and the village soon," he adds. "Those were the terms of the agreement."

"The skins came here by boat," I say. "Why can't the leather leave here the same way? There must be other towns along the coast."

"No." Demarchia is adamant. "We don't want middlemen. Why should they see all the profit from our labour?"

I arch my eyebrows at Nicanor. *Our labour? We're the ones doing the work*, is what my eyebrows state.

"How many skins can one boat take?" I ask. "We could commission one of the fishermen to take us to other port cities and sell the skins ourselves. No middleman."

"Watch this one, Rabba," says Demarchia. "He'll murder us in our sleep and before you know it we'll be the ones working for him, slaving away in those pits."

"Not if we're dead, because he'll have killed us," says Rabba, not following.

She tosses her head dismissively at him and turns to me. "I always said you were trouble," she says, but she's smiling. "I think you might be right. There are three sizeable towns and with one boat... Come, Rabba, let's make calculations."

The next morning we see Rabba walking along the bay to where the fishermen beach their boats and we realize that he's serious about this idea. That evening he discusses the different ports and which route to take. Demarchia rules out the town north of my village as the tanners there probably have even more skins than we do.

"No, if we're going to commission a boat, then we might as well go right over to the furthest towns, where there'll be better business opportunities and no leather glut," she says firmly. "What?" she says as Rabba stares at her. "You think you're the only one who can find these things out? Women talk too."

According to Demarchia's calculations, if we tighten our belts over the rest of winter – which means no more trips into the city – then we should have most of the skins ready by spring; and the more we have ready, the better our profit margins. "We can even ask Parmenas or Timon if they have spare skins they'd like to sell us. No one say anything to them until nearer the time, though, as we don't want them getting the same idea," says Demarchia, who has assumed leadership of this scheme.

The following day Rabba comes out to the vine, which has lost all its leaves now, as we scrape skins under it. I assume he's come to inspect our work, but then notice the shabby, patched tunic he's wearing and the broken sword blade in his hand. "Go on," he says to me, waving me towards the pits. "I'm not wading into any piss pits. I'll finish this one; you can start on another."

With no trading, it seems Demarchia has ordered her husband to join us doing some actual work. Usually, me and Nicanor enjoy working in companionable silence, but Rabba feels the need to talk. For the most part he just talks at us. I don't know how he can fill hours with words and yet, by the end of each evening, I can't remember a thing he's said. Sometimes he asks us questions, though. A few days later he asks Nicanor whether I'm still having nightmares. I am. Nicanor nods and this leads Rabba into a long monologue about the different temples he's been to and which gods would be the best to petition for good dreams.

"So, which temple are you going to visit?" he asks finally. "Have you thought about an offering?"

"What am I going to offer?" I say. "You've got all my wages." He concedes that this is indeed true and seems about to launch into one of his favourite topics – the avarice of priests – when I interrupt.

"I've never told you how I got that manacle, or my scars," I say.

"You don't have to," says Nicanor quietly. He knows that anything said in Rabba's presence may as well be proclaimed in the city market.

"I think I do," I say. "That's what he asked me to do. I should go throughout the region and tell people what he did for me."

"Who are you talking about?" says Rabba. He's stopped scraping.

"Before I tell you, I want you to know that this means I'm trusting you. If they find me here or know that I'm still alive, I could be the one you pass on your way to market, nailed on one of those poles."

I begin to tell them what happened. This is the third time I've explained everything and I'm grateful that no one punches me midway through. It's easier to talk about the hard times when I'm just focused on the skins in front of me that I'm scraping and not having to watch their reactions. I probably tell them more than I meant to, about how much I miss my family and how Tehinah helped me. And then I find myself saying words I hadn't even realized were an unspoken plan inside my head. "So, this is why I don't think I should stay here much longer. You're still the nearest city to my village and there must be soldiers still garrisoned here who I hurt, and hurt badly. Even if I stay out of sight, one day someone will recognize me. There's something else, too; I need to find the Master. That's why I'm so keen to sail with you to the north shore. You see, once we've sold our skins and I have my wages, I don't think I'll be coming back. I need to find out more about the man who gave me my life back, and I need to figure out what to do with it. He's from the north."

"I've heard plenty of stories about him myself," says Rabba. "But it's just bathhouse and tavern gossip. I don't believe any of it."

"What about me? Do you believe me?" I ask. Rabba looks uncomfortable and says nothing. I see Nicanor nods slightly.

"Well," says Rabba, sighing good-naturedly, "Demarchia will miss having Trouble around. Still, once we've sold all these skins there won't be much for you to do."

Nicanor doesn't comment on what we've spoken about but insists we brave the lake after work, not just for a wash but for a swim, followed by a run to warm ourselves up. I know it's his way of saying that he'll miss me. In the evening Demarchia serves us chicken broth.

"She'd almost stopped laying," she says, as she places a bowl with a generous portion of meat in it before me. "We'll need to fatten you up for your journey." Of course, Rabba has told her.

For the next three moons, little happens other than sleeping, eating and working. I've given up on returning to the city or to the public baths, and make do with quick dips in the lake and warming some water to shave my straggly beard with. Life could feel monotonous but it doesn't, because I know how much I'll miss the tannery and these people who've become an odd sort of family for me. I'm good at tanning now, and I know what each day will bring, which is comforting in a way. But I also know that life can't remain like this forever. I need more answers, and I need to know whether I can ever stop running, or if I can ever go back. Despite everything, I ache for my family, and the bond between us is something that can never be broken.

Leaves begin to bud on the vine overhead as we work on the last few skins. Demarchia has prepared food for us, and offerings are made to their gods. My prayer is still the same: *Help me find him.*

Our departure is delayed by two days because of storms, but then finally I'm carrying bales of skins above my head, tied up with string, out to a fishing boat with two crew on board. Nicanor heaves them out of my grasp and stacks them evenly to keep the boat's balance. It gradually sits deeper in the water as we bring out bale after bale. My teeth are chattering from the cold water by the time we've finished. Demarchia won't be coming with us, as someone needs to look after the tannery and the chickens. Once I've waded out to the boat with a bundle of my clothes, Nicanor jumps overboard and we wade back, ready to say goodbye. I carry a waist cloth over my head, putting it on before I say my farewells. I never did lose my bashfulness in front of Demarchia, unlike Nicanor and Rabba who stand naked beside me.

"Well, we're sad to see you go, Trouble," says Demarchia, and smiles, brushing away tears. "You look after these two and make sure they stay well away from trouble and don't go drinking away our profits, or worse." She hugs me and then Nicanor, and we head back to the boat as she berates her husband one last time. "I've done my calculations," we hear her say. "So don't go thinking I won't know if you've been spending."

We haul Rabba on board as he rolls his eyes at his wife. Still, I can tell he's going to miss her. I've never seen him leave the tannery for more than a day. The crew lower the sail and we're soon gliding away from the bay. It's a sunny day, but as the wind picks up we all put on cloaks over our tunics, feeling the chill off the water.

"I can help," I say to the fishermen. "I was going to be an apprentice once."

They introduce themselves and from their accents we can

hear that they're from the north shore. They say that they don't need help just now. I want to ask them if they know the Master, but they're busy with the sails and the rudder so I decide to wait. Nicanor wedges himself between two bales of skins, sheltering from the wind and looking pale and miserable.

"You can't be seasick," I say. "You're a swimmer."

He just looks up at me and a moment later vomits over the side of the boat. Although the winds are good, they're not in the direction we want, so we have to tack across the lake, heading so far from the shore that we can only just make it out. Clouds pass over the sun and the wind picks up, and before we know it we're being tossed around by waves growing in size. Poor Nicanor keeps retching, although he has nothing left to heave up. I help Rabba secure the skins as the boat bucks and dips in the choppy waters. It rains, and we're soon all soaked and huddled in the bottom of the boat. Even I'm feeling queasy now. Then the wind begins to gust with less insistence, and the waves start to calm, and quicker than I'd have expected, the storm eases. We've been blown off course and are actually quite near my village. I can just make it out in the distance. Part of me wishes we could just sail into the fishermen's bay, but another part of me shudders as I think of all that happened in the caves.

The fishermen make the most of the winds and we pick up speed, tacking towards the north. I fall asleep for a little while and when I wake, the sun is beginning to set. Rabba is already eating the food Demarchia packed for us, so I join him. We manage to get Nicanor to eat a little, but he soon throws it up again. We're still nowhere near the north shore. I clamber over to one of the fishermen.

"Will people understand us on the north shore?" I ask him.

He nods. "They have their own language and they don't like mixing with us, but they speak our language too." Rabba is up on the prow with the other fisherman, and Nicanor seems to have fallen asleep among the skins.

"I've never been to the north shore," I continue. "But I've heard about the holy man who can cure anyone and who has power over spirits." The fisherman smiles sardonically. "So, you know of him?" I ask.

"Where do you think I got this boat?" he says. "A few years back he came through our town collecting followers, and some of the fishermen just upped and left. Their relatives wanted to sell and I wanted to buy."

"What can you tell me about him? Does he live in your town?"

The fisherman shakes his head. "He's always travelling, but he comes through pretty often. They say that this is his base. Last I heard he was heading to the capital." Rabba comes over and starts talking about what the girls there will be like, and I don't get to ask any more questions. I have plenty, though. If I want to find the Master, how will I know which town to search for him in? If he has gone down to the capital, will I have to make that journey as well? Will my wages last for the journey? What will I do once the money runs out? Somehow I'd just assumed that I'd find the Master along the north shore. I try not to feel too despondent, but fail. I look out at the waves, wondering what I'm trying to achieve.

As the sun sets, we see other boats approaching us. They're full of nets and crew, heading out for a night's fishing. We can make out the hills of the north shore ahead, silhouetted in the evening light. We draw closer and strip, plunging into the water and carrying the bales over to the beach.

"Welcome to our town," says the fisherman in the water. "We would offer you our homes for the night, but we'll be heading out with the crew." He nods towards a group of men approaching the boat. "There are inns, but most of them are run by the others, and they won't take you," the fisherman adds to Rabba.

Rabba nods, although I don't really understand. "If you can get us firewood, we'll camp here on the bay," he says.

We finish unloading and build the piles of skins in a circle around where we'll sleep and where we hope to have a fire. We're all still a bit damp, and it's going to be a cold night. The fishermen return with bundles of firewood and a few skins of wine, and Rabba pays them. We watch as their crew join them and they push off back into the waters. Our two must already be exhausted.

I make a fire and in its flickering light, Nicanor looks pale but seems to be feeling better, and even manages to eat a little. We lay down a few skins on the sand and huddle together for warmth, our cloaks draped over us.

I wake at dawn scrabbling violently around me. Nicanor is making soothing noises. "Sorry," I say, and sit up, trying to calm my breathing. It didn't rain during the night, but we're still wet with dew.

Rabba returns from a search for a latrine and then leaves again in search of a donkey owner to take us to market. He's in a bad mood when he comes back, swearing under his breath about these cock-cutters and their stupid laws. Apparently there was only one person willing to haul the skins of pigs and Rabba is not happy with the price. We load the donkeys up and then out for the market. Rabba looks anxious and it occurs to me that if he had trouble finding someone willing to haul pigskins, we might find it equally difficult to find leatherworkers who'll be interested in buying them.

We don't know whether to take all the skins with us, or not. Will we manage to sell them all here, or have to commission another boat to travel on to the next towns? In the end, no one wants to be left watching bales all morning, so we haul everything with us.

The market is near the river, which widens as it approaches the lake. It isn't as large as the City of Horses' bazaar, which is the only market I have to compare it to, apart from the little collection of stalls in my own village. I'm reassured to see plenty of leather goods on display, and the leatherworking section is similar in size to the one where we usually sell our skins. Rabba asks the donkey owner to remain while we unload just one bale. Rabba selects a few of the best skins, which he takes around with him to the different workshops. He doesn't stay long enough to haggle with any of them, looking more and more disgusted as he moves from one to the next. I glance at Nicanor, who remains inscrutable. If we can't sell even one skin, this will be a disaster. We don't even have money to get us back to the tannery. Finally he tries a workshop on the other side of the street and takes longer inside, eventually emerging with a quick wink at us. The man behind him can't believe the quantity of skins we have with us. He calls the other leather masters from his side of the street, and five or six of them come out to see our bales.

We stay in the background, letting Rabba do the haggling. I sidle quietly up to the donkey owner. "How many bales do you think we could sell?"

"We're not a great city," he says, "but we do export a lot of our leather goods. If the price is right and they all decide to buy, you might sell at least half."

The haggling is extensive and I wander off to find a piss-pot beside one of the taverns, feeling happy as I aim into the pot that I'm helping a tanner somewhere. Rabba is still haggling hard when I get back and by now bales are opened and the leatherworkers are rooting through our goods. I'm thirsty and hungry. Eventually Rabba concludes business. Over two-thirds of the skins are taken away. The donkey driver is keen to leave in search of more business, but Rabba is soon haggling with him to take us overland to the next town, arguing that his beasts will be less heavily burdened now and able to travel further. I just help Nicanor retie the bales and position them on the animals, trying to ignore my growling stomach.

Once we're loaded up and a pouch of coins is handed to Rabba, we head back through the market. I have a growing sense of unease, but I'm not sure why and think it must be because I'm in need of breakfast.

"That fresh bread smells good," I say, as we pass a bakery. Rabba ignores me and waits until we're out of the market before he cackles in triumph and holds up the impressively large pouch of coins.

"What do you want bread for?" he asks. "Let's get ourselves some meat. It's time to feast like kings!"

We find a tavern set up beneath some large trees with smoke wafting from skewers of fish and mutton resting over charcoal, fanned vigorously by a boy. The donkey owner grumbles about the delay until we agree to bring him over some skewered fish as he watches his animals. I even join Rabba and Nicanor drinking watered-wine as I'm so thirsty and that's all they have. We're soon mopping up the meat juices dribbling down our chins with pieces of flatbread.

In some ways I feel better now that my belly is full, but that sense of unease is still there, and instead of ignoring it, I try to figure out why I feel this way. I've been feeling like this ever since the fisherman told me that the Master was probably not here right now. Somehow I just assumed that I'd find him here. Does this mean I should still stay? If I did, where would I live and what would I do, and how long would it be before the Master returned? I could go with Rabba and Nicanor to the next town, but how can I leave here without at least searching out one of his followers? I hadn't realized how hard it would be to track him down.

I clear my throat, trying to think of the right words. "Uncle Rabba," I say, and he snorts at this formal address. "I'm... I'm not coming with you."

Rabba looks crestfallen. "I didn't think we'd be parting until we'd sold all the skins," he says. "I thought, maybe far away from home, we could finally persuade you to join us with the local girls, didn't I, Nic?"

"I need to stay here. This is where I'm most likely to find the Master. He uses the town as his base. I'll see if I can find some work in a tannery or something. I just can't leave yet."

Rabba nods and Nicanor refuses to meet my eye, suddenly consumed with eating his meal. Rabba tries to be light-hearted, telling us that the price he got for the skins means we've made a decent profit. "There aren't many tanneries around here," he says, drawing out his bulging money pouch, "which helped our prices but won't help your work prospects much. You'll be needing your wages. Demarchia already did the calculations, including what you asked me to look after for you. That said, we've made more than she'd hoped, so you'll get a bonus."

He counts out more coins than I was expecting. I don't have a money pouch to put them in and end up emptying my shaving kit into my satchel and using the pouch to store the coins. He leaves an extra coin or two on the uneven planks of the table we've been sitting at, and then gives me a fierce hug, his balding head only coming up to my shoulders.

"I hope you find this Master of yours," he says, his voice catching. "Tehinah said that you were a good boy; that you just needed to discover that for yourself. I think he was right."

I hadn't realized how hard this would be. I remember when all I wanted was a new start where no one knew me, but now they know about me and they still treat me like family. Nicanor says nothing, but grabs me in a fierce embrace that lasts a long time. "You've been like a brother to me," I whisper. "I will miss you so much. You didn't care who I was or where I'd come from you just accepted me." I want to say more, but I've started crying.

He kisses my cheek, rubs angrily at a stray tear of his own and then says, "Remember me when you swim."

I think about walking with them to the limits of the town, but it feels too painful and prolonged a parting. I just stand by the roadside, crying unashamedly as the donkeys plod off, wisps of dust puffing up from their hooves and the remaining bales swaying at their sides.

"Now what do I do?" I whisper, once they're out of sight and I've blown snot from my nostrils into the dust. It's a prayer of sorts. I wander back into this strange town where I don't know anyone. There is no note of introduction in my satchel and I don't really have a plan. I hear snatches of conversation from people I pass and half the time it's in a language I don't even understand. My being here seems so futile now, and yet I'm surprised at the determination I feel bubbling up inside me. I will find him.

Chapter Thirteen

I decide to wander back to the market and just see what happens. Without the donkeys to watch or bales of skins to sell, I find that this time I really look around and notice things. I still don't know how to identify which people are of the same religion as the Master. I think back to my initial encounter with him and his followers. They all had longer hair than most people I'm used to, but maybe I was imagining it, or it had nothing to do with their religion. How will I find him?

My satchel feels heavy with the weight of coins and I hear them clinking as I walk. I wonder if others also recognize that sound and for the first time I feel worried about thieves and pickpockets. I'm nearing the market now, but instead of continuing, I turn around and head up towards the hills. I follow a main path, leaving the town behind, until I pass two dusty pines which have grown unusually close together. They make a distinctive landmark and I look around for a good hiding place. It's almost noon and there's no one else around. Seventeen paces away from the trees are some rocks. I manage to lift one, take some coins out of my satchel, along with my shaving stuff, and place the satchel and cloak in a crevice, covering it again with the rock.

Hair length might not help me, but it should be pretty obvious who is circumcised in the baths, and that's where I'm heading. That way, if I do find some of the Master's followers, at least I won't still smell like a tanner. I ask for directions and pass back through the market. The baths are fed by water from the river. I pay my entrance fee, hand my clothes to an attendant and then head into the steam room. It's not as grand as the baths in the City of Horses but I enjoy the whole process just as much. Once I'm washed, shaved and oiled, I wander out into the main courtyard, shielding my eyes from the glare of the sun on the floor tiles.

By now I think I've figured out who is circumcised and who isn't. Most of the men in the courtyard are either wrestling or watching, and they're not circumcised. There's a group of old men with long beards who look religious but not particularly friendly. The only other people around are two young men sitting apart under the shade of a tree, and from here I can't tell if they're circumcised or not. I wander over towards them.

"Do you mind if I join you in the shade?" I ask, smiling. They glance briefly at each other and look uncomfortable.

"We can't sit with you," says one of them, after noting that I'm not circumcised. I can tell from the way he speaks that this is not his first language.

"Here," says the other, getting up and gesturing at the bench so that I can sit down. I can see he's circumcised. "We'll just stand for a while in the sun."

I'd heard that they keep separate from us but I hadn't realized just how strict they were. It makes me more confused because the Master didn't seem to care about this at all. "No, keep your seat," I say. "I only wanted to ask you something. If I stand over here, is that far enough?"

The man who offered to stand smiles apologetically as he sits again. He's strikingly handsome. The other, skinny, younger-looking one, just gives his friend a look which says: *You don't need to apologize.* I don't like him.

"I… I was hoping you can help me," I say to the politer of the two. "I'm looking for someone from around here. He's a holy man who can do impossible things. He even has power over spirits. Actually, he rescued me from this." I point at my scars. They've faded a bit now but they're still visible. "I heard that he sometimes comes here and I want to find him again. I have so many questions."

"We call him the teacher," says the handsome one.

"You do?" I try not to appear too eager. I'm about to sit down next to him but then remember that I can't. They still seem quite concerned about me.

"He's one of our people. He didn't come for you," says the thin one.

"Yes, he did," I say, trying to keep the anger out of my voice. "He crossed a lake and came through a storm for me." I stare hard at them, daring them to challenge me. They say nothing and just look worried. I sigh in annoyance. "I've been searching for him for a long time."

"Listen," says the nicer one. He speaks with a hushed urgency. "We follow him, but he has enemies. We can't talk here. Head towards the hills out of town and you'll see twin pines." I nod, not mentioning that all my stuff is hidden up there. "Meet us there. We'll leave now and you follow a bit later."

"Thank you," I say.

"Malchus," the man says. "My name is Malchus. Now go and pretend you're interested in the wrestling."

I nod and wander over to the arena section of the courtyard. A few youths are marking out a race track and I'm tempted to see if I can join them. Then I remember how I shouldn't be drawing attention to myself. I watch the games, but all I can think about is that soon I will be talking with someone who actually knows the Master. Finally I'll get answers to some of my questions. Perhaps they can tell me where the Master is now. I wait a little longer and then go back to the changing rooms.

As I put on my tunic I wonder why the followers seemed so reluctant to talk to me – to talk with anyone, for that matter, off by themselves under the shade. I can't imagine how the Master would have enemies, but then I remember the pigs and my village and wonder what kind of reception he would get if he ever showed up there again.

These are my thoughts as I walk towards the hills, pausing briefly at an aqueduct to scoop a drink of water. I find the two men waiting for me under the pines.

"You didn't tell us your name," says Malchus, as I approach.

"I'm Phineas," I explain. It'll be nice not to be known as Trouble.

"I'm Eleazar," says the skinny one. I haven't heard a name like this before and I repeat it, trying to get the right pronunciation.

"We meant no offence before," says Malchus. "It's just that you're the first outsider we've met who follows the teacher."

So, I'm an outsider.

"I don't follow him," I say. "I wanted to, but he wouldn't let me. I only met him once, briefly, but he still changed my life. He gave it back to me. Now I want to find him and learn more."

Malchus nods. "Why don't you sit on that rock there, and we'll sit over here, and then you can tell us what happened."

"It might take some time," I say. "I should probably tell you how I came to be filled with spirits in the first place."

So I do. They ask a few questions, but mainly they keep quiet. I get lost in my story. At one point I look up as I'm explaining how the village tried to poison me, and I see that Malchus has tears on his cheeks. Even the thin one, Eleazar, seems moved. It's only when I come to the point where I describe the storm that suddenly stopped that Malchus interrupts.

"Have you ever wondered why the storm stopped so suddenly?" he asks. I hadn't. "It was him, the teacher, the Master. He stilled it. I remember Cephas telling me."

"Cephas," I say. "Yes, he rescued me from drowning. But that comes later." They ask me more questions now, particularly Eleazar, who seems to have a hard time believing that the Master would take me in his arms.

"It's against our law. Surely the teacher knows that."

"I didn't ask him to embrace me," I say. "If I was him, I wouldn't have wanted to touch me. I was filthy and I stank."

I tell them about seeing my mother again, and I cry. Then I talk about escaping and trying to find out more about the Master in the City of Horses. I end up voicing something I've tried hard for all this time not to think about. "I'm free now. The spirits have gone, but I still don't feel free. I'll always be bound to the things I've done. I can't un-kill Aqub or un-harm all those people in my village and the soldiers."

"He can forgive sins," says Malchus quietly.

"But it wasn't him that I hurt; it was all these other people, and if my own mother can't forgive me, I'm not holding out much hope."

"I don't understand it either," says Malchus, "but I've seen it. Just after the teacher cured me, when he was still here in our town, everyone wanted to hear what he had to say, even the religious lot. He was speaking in our prayer house and the place was packed. So packed that a group of youths climbed on the roof and took away the tiles and lowered their friend down so he could meet the teacher. The boy was paralysed. The teacher told him that his sins were forgiven. You can imagine the response from the priests. They all protested that no one but God can forgive sins. The teacher asked what was harder: to forgive the boy or make him walk. Then he told the boy to get up and he did."

I'm silent for a moment. "I have to find him," I whisper. "That's why I came here. Finding him has been my constant prayer."

"To which gods?" asks Eleazar.

"I don't really know. I just pray to the God of the Master and hope the prayer goes to the right place."

Malchus gets up and comes towards me. "Brother Phineas," he says, "the teacher can forgive you. You can be free." Then he kisses me on the cheek and embraces me.

"Malchus," Eleazar protests.

"What? If the teacher called him brother, who are we to say otherwise? I don't care if he's not circumcised." He turns to me. "I'll tell you properly some other time how the teacher changed my life. You might not believe me if you hadn't experienced him yourself, but I was once a leper. No one would touch me or come near me. I knew what it was to feel the sting of stones when villagers chased me away, or the flinch and the revulsion of someone normal if I came too close. According to our law, if a healthy man touches someone like me, he also becomes dirty, contaminated. But the teacher, he touched me and instead of me infecting him, he infected me. I was infected by his wellness. He made me clean and whole again, just like he did you. Phineas, I think God has brought you to us for a reason. I'm glad you didn't give up on us in the baths when we appeared rude. Just know that our own situation isn't that great right now. I'll explain more later."

"Malchus is right," says Eleazar quietly. "I'm sorry. I still have too much of the old way in me." He stands up and comes towards me. "I... I've never done this before," he says and embraces me awkwardly, then looks at me as if expecting gratitude.

"Why are you people like this, separating yourselves from everyone else?" I say. I'm not sure if I'm more baffled or just angry.

Malchus puts an arm around my shoulder and pats my chest affectionately. "You're right, we do love all our rules. But the teacher is showing us a new way. You know that's what we call ourselves? *The Way*. And now you, you're part of this new way. We just need a little time to get used to that." Malchus looks up at the afternoon sun. "Brother Phineas, when you met us, we were bathing in preparation for our most important religious feast. My family will be waiting for us. I'm sorry I can't invite you."

"Is that because I'm not one of you?"

Malchus nods, looking serious. "I don't think this is right and meeting you today has convinced me even more. The teacher told us he's come for everyone, but I don't think we want to hear that. It's one of the reasons our religious people hate him. Phineas, I want you to stay with me at my house, but I've only just returned here and my father isn't a follower of The Way. I know he won't allow someone who isn't one of us to stay. Already he's taking a risk having Eleazar stay with us."

"Why? Did you do something wrong?"

"No, but Eleazar threatens them, the religious authorities. I'll explain more later." Malchus continues, "We went to the baths because our people don't usually frequent them and it's one of the few places we can visit. The only reason we talked to you at all was because we saw that you weren't circumcised and weren't one of them." Instead of answering my questions, Malchus is just giving me a whole load more. "So, we've never had someone enter our house who isn't part of our religion, and I can't make trouble there tonight, not during our most holy festival."

I'm not very impressed with their religion. "I have money for an inn, but if you have a relative or friend who might offer me a bed for the night…" They exchange another awkward look. Then I remember this morning with the leatherworkers; one side of the street unwilling to do business with us, but the other side happy to trade. How do these people with their two different religions live together in the same town and yet have so little to do with each other? I toss my head in dismissal. "I'll sleep here. Go to your feast."

"Phineas," says Malchus, looking helpless.

Eleazar takes off his cloak and hands it to me. "I'm sorry — it's not much," he says.

"We'll come back tomorrow morning and bring food with us," Malchus adds, handing me his cloak as well. I want to throw them both in the dust and just get out of this stupid town and catch up with Rabba and Nicanor. They treated me better than this and they aren't even followers of the Master.

"You might know more about the Master than I do," I say, trying to keep my voice even. "But even in the short time I spent with him, I know that he was never like this."

Malchus sighs. "You're right," he says. "I'll try to explain more tomorrow. There's still a lot you don't know about our situation."

I just shrug and turn away from them. I'm furious. My village had good reason to keep away from me. I was dangerous, wild and unpredictable. Even in the City of Horses, I could understand if people wrinkled their nose as I passed, still carrying with me the odour of the tannery. But this? To be unwelcome and considered dirty just because of who I am; something I have no control over? I don't know if I even want to see them tomorrow. I wonder if they'll have to wash their cloaks after I've slept on them. I've heard a few people speak with derision about the people of the north shore, but I had no idea that this was what they were really like. Can the Master really be from this people?

Maybe that's why his own people hate him so much. He's so different. I realize that I can't leave now, not with so many unanswered questions. I need to know more about The Way. As I think about it, I realize that neither of them has embraced someone like me before; someone not part of their religion. Perhaps I was too hard on them. It seems they're still figuring out what this new way is as well.

I start praying, and this time I pray to the God of The Way. I ask him to help me and guide me. Then I go over to the rock pile and take a few extra coins from my satchel. I could probably find a tavern in town with rooms for my people, but with the extra cloaks, I decide to save money and sleep outside. I'm hungry, though, and head back towards the town in search of stalls still open. I can hear singing from some of the houses and the heady smell of roast lamb wafts through the air. Eventually I spot the flickering light of a clay lamp and find a small stall selling dried figs, almonds, raisins, and olives. The woman selling there is one of us; I can hear it in her accent. She folds my purchase into a wide, thin flatbread and hands it to me. My fingers brush against hers when I hand her the money and this doesn't bother her.

Look at me, I'm not even here a day and already it's "us" and "them".

I use my satchel as a makeshift pillow. The ground is stony and uncomfortable and it takes me a long time to sleep. When I do, I sleep fitfully. The next morning I wake up with my hand around Malchus's throat. His face is red and his eyes bulge and behind him Eleazar has lifted up a stone and is about to dash it at my head. I let go as soon as I realize where I am, and Malchus coughs and clutches at his throat.

"I'm sorry, I'm so sorry," I say. "It's the nightmares. I have them every night. If you ever have to wake me again, remember you need to keep your distance."

"I'll remember that. I'll definitely remember that," Malchus croaks, smiling weakly. "I thought maybe you were still angry about last night."

"I am," I say. "If you came to my village, I would never dream of you staying anywhere but my house. It doesn't matter what your religion is."

"Listen," says Malchus. "We should really still be at home for our festival and the noon meal, but we came here because we want you to know more about the teacher. We have an idea about how you might be able to stay in my father's house, but we can talk about that later." I glance up and see that I must have slept away the morning. "You still haven't had breakfast," Malchus continues. "Let's eat, and then maybe we can tell you more about how the teacher changed our lives."

Chris Aslan

He takes one of the cloaks I slept on and spreads it under the tree in the shade, laying out dried crackers, dried fish, a small woven basket filled with chunks of cold roasted lamb and bitter herbs. Eleazar produces dried figs and dates. Then he thanks God for the food and we eat. Malchus tells me how he was born in this town and worked as a fish-dryer. I tell him that this is also my family's profession. He was happily married when his wife discovered his illness. Soon he was banished to a leper colony and his wife married another man. Although I never married Berenice, it seems we have a lot in common. As he describes his experiences of being a leper – nothing but an object of pity and disgust – I see the similarities grow. "And so I left the lake to go south and get as far away from my heartache as possible. I met Shimon, Eleazar's father, also a leper, and we became friends."

Eleazar then explains what he went through after his father contracted the disease and how he and his sisters were left to fend for themselves. He tried to find meaning in religion and even joined a militant group seeking to overthrow the occupation. "Our religion and its laws were the most important thing to us. The law was where I found my identity. It's taking me time to leave behind these old ways and embrace the way of the teacher," he finishes sheepishly. I don't interrupt; I want to hear more. Knowing that they've suffered too makes me feel more kindly disposed towards them.

Malchus describes how close to death he was, and his grief at losing Shimon. Then he finally found the teacher and the teacher cured him. "And not just me. I helped a boy from the mountains meet the teacher. He was completely paralysed from the neck down, but the teacher touched him and then he was up on his feet and running around with the whole town in uproar!"

Even though I saw what the Master did with the spirits in me, it's still hard to believe what I'm hearing. How can a mere man have so much power? The Master must be a son of one of the gods.

Eleazar interrupts and describes his first encounter with the teacher, and then tells me what it was like to follow him and watch him do incredible things. "And Phineas, the teacher isn't afraid to make enemies, particularly among our religious leaders. We've always believed that our God is only interested in religious people, but they're the ones the teacher speaks against. He eats with whores and collaborators and even with people like you: outsiders."

"I hope you'll do the same," I say. I haven't quite forgiven them for their lack of hospitality last night. I'm also in a strange mood and I don't know why.

"If you knew what my village is like, you'd understand," says Eleazar. He describes what life is like there, and how he and his sisters are ostracized by many of their own neighbours, even after the wonders the whole village has witnessed the teacher do. Then Eleazar tells me about his death. I almost laugh in disbelief. I've heard of people recovering from serious fevers but no one has ever died and then come alive again. Malchus assures me that it's true and that he was there.

"Are you sure you haven't confused the facts since this happened?" I ask.

"Why is it so difficult for you to believe after what the teacher did for you?" asks Eleazar. "Who ever heard of a man having the strength to snap iron chains or defeat so many soldiers single-handedly? And what I'm talking about didn't happen to me a long time ago, it happened last week!"

They explain how the religious authorities are now after the teacher and want to kill him because of the threat they think he poses. "It's jealousy," says Eleazar. "And control. They want all the control themselves."

"They're afraid of the teacher's power and Eleazar is living proof of that. That's why we had to flee here, further from the capital and where things are a bit quieter," Malchus explains. "Everyone in the capital has heard about this boy who was brought back to life. As long as he's alive, he's a threat. We need to keep a low profile until we get word that it's safe to return. Can you see now why I can't afford to antagonize my father?"

"I don't understand," I say. I'm actually finding it hard to concentrate and I'm sweating, even though it's not hot. My mouth feels really dry. "I saw the power the Master has. If he can command spirits, why is he afraid of men? Why can't he fight them or something?"

"That's not his way," says Malchus.

"He told my sister that he came to die," says Eleazar quietly. "I don't really know what that means, but I think she understood. He talked about how a seed must fall into the ground and die before growing into a sapling."

"That can't be right. Why would he come to die? He brought me life. I've seen his power."

"I used to think mainly about his power, too," says Eleazar. "I thought he was our chosen one, predicted in our holy writings, come to lead us into battle against the foreign armies. But that's not his way."

It's as he says this that I realize I'm finding it hard to breathe. There's a tightness in my chest and a knot in my stomach. I blink and shake my head to clear it.

"Phineas?" says Eleazar.

"Something's wrong," I gasp.

"Are you ill?" says Malchus. I can barely hear him over the pounding of blood so loud in my ears. "Come on, El, give me a hand. We can't leave him here. We need to bring him home. I'll deal with my father later."

I'm too big to carry but they support my arms and I stumble forward, propped up. "My satchel," I gasp. I lean against Malchus as Eleazar picks up the cloaks and my satchel.

"Listen," says Malchus. All I can hear is my heart pounding.

"What?" says Eleazar.

"Exactly. There's no birdsong. Not even crickets chirping. What's going on?"

Although I'm sweating, I start to shiver too. Clouds obscure the sun, and a wind picks up. I don't just feel sick, there's a huge sadness, like grief, welling up inside me and I don't know why. I start to sob. I can't help myself.

"Phineas, what's happening?" says Malchus. I can hear the fear in his voice. I shake my head. I don't know. All I know is that something is terribly wrong.

"Why is it so dark?" says Eleazar. I glance up at the sky. Dark clouds are brooding but still it shouldn't be this dark. I double over in pain. Eleazar begins to speak urgently in their language. I think he's praying.

"Keep going," says Malchus. "The doctor lives on our street."

I don't know what this is, but I know it isn't something a doctor can cure. I want to tell him this but I'm struggling for breath. Then another wave of grief overpowers me and I sob and even cry out loud. We stumble on, my head down for the most part. In the town, everyone is out on the streets looking up at the darkened skies, spitting on their hearts and praying to whichever god they think might help. Street dogs howl. We pass a man trying to control a fearful and skittish mare.

"We're almost home," says Malchus, trying to sound reassuring. I can barely nod. Then we suddenly lurch over, sprawling in the dust. I look around to see who pushed us. But it's the ground beneath us; it's rippling. There are screams and people cry out, lurching and falling. We're under an apricot tree just coming into leaf and its branches shake and creak as if in a powerful wind. I still can't breathe and feel my face getting hotter. Malchus and Eleazar cry out. I glance up as the man with the nervous horse manages to drop from his saddle just before the animal buckles, whinnying in terror, and falls to the dust beside his cowering form. I start to see everything from far away, as if I'm looking out from a long dark cave, and I realize that I'm just moments from losing consciousness. Then, abruptly, the ground stops moving and I find I can breathe again. Everything is still as the dust settles, with just the sound of my panting. Then, tentatively, people clamber to their feet.

There's a sudden commotion behind a mud-brick wall as a smaller building – perhaps an open kitchen or a stable – collapses, sending up a plume of dust and bits of straw. Malchus offers me a hand and pulls me to my feet.

"Are you all right?" he asks.

I look up and see that already the sky is brightening. There are a few tentative chirps and then the birds start singing again. More than that, something feels changed inside me. I don't know how I know this, but what just happened to me and to everything around us is somehow connected to the Master.

"It's finished," is all I can say.

"Well, I don't think we need to worry about you entering our house any more," says Malchus, trying to smile. "I don't think anyone will be sleeping indoors tonight. There might be aftershocks."

Eleazar cups my elbow to support me. "Thanks, but I think I can manage," I say. And I can. I feel fine. In fact, I'm surprised at how calm and serene I feel. We turn a corner and walk a little further down the road until we come to a compound with a door in the wall. Malchus opens it and we enter.

The compounds here are much more spacious than in my village and a large mud-brick wall surrounds an orchard and a vegetable patch beside a mud-brick house with a flat roof, along with a few outbuildings, such as latrine and sheep-pen. I look around and see something that makes me happy and long for home at the same time: festooned between the trees and up on the roof are rows and rows of drying redbellies. I try to swallow the lump in my throat.

An older woman adjusts her headscarf and gets up from a wooden covered platform where she has been sitting with a bowl in her hands. She throws her arms around Malchus. She's still beautiful and the likeness between them is strong. I don't need to understand their language to know that she's saying: "Thank God you're all right. I was so worried about you."

She turns to me, and I'm pretty sure she asks, "And who's this?" She's smiling and welcoming, but I know that the smile will freeze in a moment when she finds out who and what I am. I don't know if Malchus intends to pretend I'm something or not, but if he does, I have no intention of playing along.

"My name is Phineas," I say in our language. "I'm sorry to intrude on your house. I was sick and Malchus helped me."

She says something else in their language, smiling politely but puzzled, and then turns to Malchus. He talks to her and, as I predicted, the smile disappears and she beckons him to come into the inner room with her. Then she realizes it's probably not safe, so she takes him behind a row of fig and pomegranate trees and we hear them argue in fierce whispers.

"Listen," I say to Eleazar. "I don't want to cause trouble for Malchus, or draw attention to you. I think I should go."

"Wait," he says. "We were talking earlier this morning on our way to meet you and I think there is a way you could stay here and also help Malchus assure the community that he's still one of us." Eleazar looks up at me expectantly. "You could join us."

I frown. "But I thought I already had. You know I want to follow The Way."

"No, I mean you could also join our religion. The doctor Malchus mentioned. He lives on this street. Before sundown and the start of our rest day, you could become one of us. You could be circumcised."

Chapter Fourteen

The sun has set and their rest day has begun. Or should I call it *our* rest day? I lie on generous bedding placed on the covered platform I saw before. It's an outdoor eating area, I think. Not any more. They've created screens by hanging up linen sheets to keep flies away from my wound. Cushions have been stacked up on either side of me, and draped over them is another sheet that covers me without touching my body at all. I'm sweating from the pain and my penis feels as if it's on fire. I'm thirsty but I don't want to drink anything because then I'd have to piss and the thought of that almost makes me weep.

Malchus and Eleazar, aware that I'm in no mood to talk, sit under the vine, but it's only just budding and doesn't offer much shade. I hear snippets of conversation in their language drift across, and every now and then recognize one of our words that they use for things like "baths".

When Eleazar asked me if I'd consider circumcision, the last thing I expected to say was "yes". It seemed a pretty high price for a bed for the night. I argued that I know virtually nothing about their religion and that I'm not even sure I want to be part of it. Eleazar pointed out that their God is the same God the teacher calls Father. This was new to me. When the Master told me about his Father, I hadn't realized that he was talking about his Father being a god. So, he *is* a son of a god. This was most people's conclusion back in the baths in the City of Horses. Maybe we understand him better than his own people. Then Eleazar corrected me and said that there is only one God and that all the other gods are not real. I can't think about that now, not with this throbbing pain.

"Do you see how little I know of your religion?" I had said. "Now can you see why I'm nowhere near ready to join you?"

Malchus came over at that point and told me about the ten most important laws they have in their religion. I didn't understand all of them, especially the one about having to rest once a week, but most of them made sense. It's good not to envy, it's good to respect your parents, it's good not to kill. I'm aware that I've broken these three laws already.

"And anyway," said Malchus grinning, "you'd just be losing a piece of skin that you have no use for."

Then Eleazar got upset with Malchus for making light of something so important. Eleazar is definitely more religious than Malchus. I still felt this serenity I can't explain, and I didn't want to see them argue, so I just said yes. Yes, I would be circumcised. If I'd realized just how painful it would be, there's no way I'd have agreed.

Malchus beamed, and explained the situation to his mother. At first she seemed reluctant, but then started preparing this place for me and then offered me a large pitcher of water to drink. "If you drink plenty now and then pass water before the procedure, it will help," she said. It turns out that she and the rest of the family can also speak our language. She introduced me to her other son and his wife.

Malchus went to get the doctor. I asked Eleazar exactly what the procedure would entail, but he was unhelpfully vague and told me that none of them remember because they were babies at the time.

"But will it be painful?" I asked again.

"I'm sure you've experienced worse," he said.

Then the doctor arrived and encouraged me to pass water. Afterwards I took off my waist cloth, screened from the rest of the household, and once the doctor had examined me, I lay down and he asked Malchus to sit on my legs while Eleazar held my arms.

"Here." The doctor passed me a thick strip of leather. "Bite down on this if you need to."

I remembered the last time I had to bite down on leather in the Teller's hut, and look how that turned out.

I couldn't help looking at the instruments as he took them out of a small bag. The knife glinted and there was a wooden clamp and a small jar of some kind of powder. I planned to pay attention to what happened next as he gathered my foreskin in the clamp, but when the knife sliced down all I could do was yell and curse, grateful that the leather strip in my mouth muffled my expletives.

I almost knocked Malchus and Eleazar off me as I arched my back in agony, before whimpering quietly as the doctor put powder on the wound, stemming the blood with fluffs of raw wool. I spat the leather strip out and then vomited. Malchus smoothed my forehead with a sponge, congratulating me quietly. I just swore at him and then lay back, exhausted and bathed in sweat.

Now, as the sun sets, I'm wondering if I've done the right thing. Already people look at me in the baths, noticing my scars and wondering if I'm a slave. What will they make of me now? What if I end up going back to Rabba to work again? What will Nicanor think of me every time we strip for work and he sees what I've done? Or if I'm accepted back by my village and work with Timaeus on the boats, they'll call me *cock-cutter* and *mutilator.* I'll always be different. Even more different. I wonder if, instead of fitting in better here with Malchus and his family, now I just won't fit anywhere. Will I ever have a place to call home again, or people to call family? I still remember the words of the Master. He didn't tell me to go and get circumcised; he told me to tell everyone in my region about the mercy and goodness of God.

That's really what I want to do. I want my family, my village, our region, to know about the Master and his Father who is a god; who is God. First, though, I hope that Malchus and Eleazar can teach me more, and also that I can meet the Master again and learn from him. Will he be happy that I'm circumcised?

I probably sleep but it doesn't feel like it as even the slightest movement shifts the throbbing hurt to searing pain. Malchus and Eleazar sleep either side of me. In the morning, I have to wake Malchus to ask him how I should pee. He brings me an old clay pot and tries to help me, but it's an agonizing and humiliating experience. He brings me a pitcher and basin so that I can wash my hands and then, once the modesty sheet is in place again, his mother brings me a bowl of chicken soup which she prepared before the rest day. The doctor won't visit me until sunset, as that would be considered work. What is this strange religion I'm caught up in?

Seeing as Malchus and Eleazar have to rest as well, they spend most of the day sitting beside me and telling me about the Master. The more I learn, the stranger it seems that any of his people would be against him. They tell me how his birth was predicted many times in their holy writings, and about the different kinds of people he's helped and cured. It turns out that I'm not the first person he's set free from spirits.

Malchus's father comes to visit me at one point and officially welcomes me as a guest into their house with prayers. He also speaks our language well. I'm starting to see more of a difference between his family, who don't seem that different from any other family around the lake, and Eleazar, who comes from a village where everyone is their race and religion. I ask him how he felt when the Master cured Malchus and then I ask him what other things he knows about the Master. I tell him my story and how I've come here. I tell him that it's for the Master that I'm willing to endure this operation because all I want is to follow him. Then I ask him why he isn't also seeking after the man who cured his son. He looks a little uncomfortable and tells me that it's something he is thinking about. Malchus just sits quietly, grinning. After his father has left us, Malchus punches me gently on the shoulder. "Already you are a blessing on our house," he says.

The day passes quicker than I would have expected, and there are prayers to mark its end at sundown. Then Malchus goes to fetch the doctor, who comes and inspects my wounds. We didn't pay him yesterday and it's cost more than I'm happy about, but Eleazar has the coins from my pouch ready for him. The doctor is happy with my progress and says that by morning I should be up and walking, if a little delicately. Malchus sits beside him, unusually pale and quiet. He sees the doctor out of the house and then comes back.

Eleazar also notices. "Malchus, what's the matter?"

"It might just be a rumour. Yes, it's probably just a rumour, but I need to go to the market or the baths to find out more," he says.

"What? What rumour?" I ask.

"The doctor's neighbours were saying that the teacher was arrested on the night of the feast," says Malchus quietly. "And that they nailed him yesterday just outside the capital."

I think about the men I saw nailed to the poles beside the crossroads and I feel sick. "How can that be?" I say. "What has he ever done wrong?"

"I don't know. I don't even know if this is true or just a rumour they want us to believe."

I get that feeling in my stomach and all over me that happens when you stand on the very edge of a cliff and look over.

"I have to meet him," I whisper. "I have to ask him to forgive me."

"We don't know if any of this is even true," says Eleazar. "I don't care about the risk. I can't just stay here. Let's try to find out more."

They leave and I lie there helpless. "Please don't let him die. Don't let him be dead," I whisper as tears begin to spill. I remember the piteous moaning of the men nailed to their poles and their agonizing battle for each breath. It's too appalling to think that the best person I've ever met would suffer like that. "Don't let this be true," I pray, just repeating it over and over again, and eventually I fall into a fitful sleep.

The next day I wake up before the others. The nightmares made me thrash in my sleep, so it was the pain that woke me up. I wear my waist cloth loosely as I hobble very slowly to the latrine. It's the first time I've really explored the spacious compound. Flanking the path to the latrine are pomegranate trees. They're low – more bushes really – and covered with blood-red blossoms swelling into the beginnings of fruit. I can't help it; whenever I see pomegranate trees they remind me of our courtyard and what I did to Aqub.

It's painful when I pee and that sharpens my mind and stops me thinking, which is a good thing. As I hobble slowly away from the latrine, Pappus – Malchus's brother – arrives at the compound with two barrows of redbellies. His wife and his mother prepare buckets and knives and look up to greet me. I hobble over to them.

"We used to feed all the entrails and stuff to our neighbours' piglets," I say, smiling as I remember the way the piglets would jostle around the bucket and unless Berenice held some back, the runts of the litter would get nothing. I look up and see Pappus and his mother trying not to look disgusted. I suppose I won't get to eat pig again now. I still don't really understand why one animal is all right to eat but another isn't.

"Let me help you," I say. "I need something to do. Do you have a spare knife?" I sit beside Pappus and he doesn't move away. It's nice to finally see one benefit from circumcision. "I can't bend down, but if you're happy to keep me supplied with fish, I can gut them quickly." Chickens loiter around my feet, racing each other to the entrails we throw to them. Pappus's wife has gone to make breakfast. I ask them about the rumours and whether there's any more news.

"The fishermen were talking about it at the bay this morning," says Pappus. "No one knows what's happening. I just try to stay out of it."

"But the Master, the teacher, he cured your brother. No one else could do that. He has power from God. Surely you see that?"

Pappus looks at his mother uncomfortably. "This teacher has become really divisive," he says, "especially down at the bay. Some of his closest apprentices are fishermen I used to do business with. Since Malchus left I've been running the business alone and I need to stay out of politics and not take sides."

I want to argue with him, but I don't think it will change anything. We work in silence and then I say, "You know, my brother also took over our fish-drying business when I left." And then I tell him what happened to me. Pappus and his mother listen avidly. I get to the part where the Master set me free and explain how he accepted me. I'm not going to honey-coat it for them. I can see it makes them uncomfortable, that he was willing to touch someone who wasn't circumcised, but I want them to know that the Master cares about everyone, not just them.

By the time I've finished, we need to smoke the fish. This is something new to me as we always salted them back home. I watch as Pappus strings up clusters of fish inside a wooden room that looks like a latrine but has a brick base and a fire smouldering beneath it. He closes the door once the room is full, and adds wet wood to the fire, which takes a while to catch, and burns with a lot of smoke.

"Who knows what's happening in the capital," says Malchus ambling over to us in just his waist cloth. He's finally woken up. "Everyone's talking about it but no one knows anything. Eleazar can help me take sacks of dried fish to the wholesale market on the edge of town. It's where the first messenger horses will stop, and hopefully we can find out what exactly happened."

The doctor comes while they're gone and inspects my wound again and tugs off the raw wool, which makes me yelp and makes the wound bleed. He sprinkles on more powder and seems satisfied with the healing process.

"Usually I do babies," he says, "but you're the fourth adult I've cut." He pours something from a small glass vial into a basin and then adds water and begins washing my wound. It feels awkwardly intimate, so I'm grateful for his distracting flow of conversation. He tells me how some men convert because of marriage and some because it makes sense to them that there is just one God. "Do you know why I agreed to this operation?" I ask. He looks up, curious. It's the second time in one day that I've told others about the Master and what he did for me. He listens and at the end he says that for a while he was worried that the Doctor would put him out of business, because he was able to cure all diseases as well as banish spirits. He's also heard the rumours from the capital but doesn't know any more than the rest of us.

Malchus comes back in the afternoon as I doze on my sleeping mat, with the rest of the family sleeping inside the house. "It's true," Malchus says, before I can even ask. "He died on Friday afternoon."

I feel numb.

"They say that the skies got really dark in the capital and all over. It sounds like even the foreign soldiers were spooked by it.

They speared him to make sure he was dead, and then he was put in a cave of the dead." He sighs, wiping his hands over his face, and then sobs. "I don't know what we're supposed to do now."

"How can this be?" I whisper, and Malchus squats down beside me and we weep together. After a while I look up. "Where's Eleazar?"

"He wanted to be alone," says Malchus, "but I knew you'd want to hear the news."

I don't know why we don't cry more, but both of us just sit there in silence, not really thinking. Just feeling numb. I'm not sure how long we sit like that before Eleazar returns.

We look up, wondering why Eleazar looks so determined. "This isn't the end," he says. "Think how long I was dead for. Everyone had given up on me, but that wasn't the end. If the teacher could bring me back from death, then he can do the same with himself." Malchus and I look at each other. Eleazar sighs in exasperation. "My sisters understood. They knew he was willingly going to his death – that's why they broke the jar of spikenard. He could have come with us up here. We've seen him melt into the crowd enough times before. He told us that a seed must fall and die before it can grow. He told us, Malchus!"

We're silent for a moment and then I speak. "When I had the spirits inside me, I could defeat a whole section of soldiers. I could break chains. I was full of so much power, I couldn't even control it; it controlled me. The Master was more powerful than those spirits. I remember that power. Malchus, how did it feel when he touched you and you felt the sickness leave you?"

Malchus nods.

"I don't understand this," says Eleazar, "but I know that it's not the end."

The next few days are awful. We're waiting but we don't know what we're waiting for or how long to wait. I think we should go straight down to the capital but there's no way I could travel with my wound, and I'd hate for them to leave me here, so I say nothing. It's probably harder for Malchus and Eleazar as they try not to go out much or attract attention. At least I'd be cooped up here anyway, recovering.

Although we three sleep outside, the compound feels a bit small for all of us and I have an altercation with Pappus. I can walk around now, as long as I do so slowly, and I catch him rooting through my satchel.

"What are you doing?" I ask, and he looks up guiltily.

"It was my father," he says. "He asked me to."

"Asked you to do what? Steal from me?"

"No, no, nothing like that. It's against our law to steal. No, he wanted me to just make sure that you hadn't brought idols or amulets into our house."

"Did you hear me when I told you what happened to me?" I ask, trying not to get angry. "It was gods and amulets that left me filled with spirits and imprisoned in my own body."

"I know. I'm sorry," he begins. "We just have to be careful about these things."

He probably says more, but I've already walked away. I decide to leave the compound, even if I'm taking a risk.

I wander to the market. I'd like to go to the baths, but my wound, although healing nicely, is still an angry red and a little too conspicuous. I meander through it and down to the lake. Walking along the shore, I find a deserted area, strip and wade into the water. I don't know if the doctor would approve, but the coldness of the water feels so good against my skin and soon I'm swimming slowly. My muscles have missed exercise and I go further along the shore than I meant to. As I swim back I notice with annoyance that a group of fishermen have made a fire near my sandals and pile of clothes.

I wade out of the water. One or two of them glance at my fresh scar. One day I hope that all my scars will fade enough for me not to be a curiosity. One of them calls out to me, but I don't understand. I put on my waist cloth and sandals and wander over.

"I don't understand you," I say in my language.

"Oh, I thought you were one of us," he says, switching languages.

"What do you want?" I ask.

"It doesn't matter," says the fisherman. "We're just talking."

"Why? Is there news?" I ask, trying to keep my voice even. "What's the latest from the capital?"

"They can't find his body. It's gone, and people are saying they've seen him alive," says one of them, and two others snigger derisively.

"The authorities are telling people not to believe anything, but they can't show the body to prove he's still dead."

"Everyone's taken leave of their senses," says another. "It'll all blow over soon."

I don't hear more because I'm already heading back to Malchus's compound to see what he's heard. He's not there and nor is Eleazar. It must be true, I reason to myself. We know the Master has power over death. I imagine him riding into this town with his followers, and me falling at his feet, letting him know that I'm now circumcised and I'll do anything he wants as long as he'll let me stay with him and be his follower. I almost start crying just thinking about it.

"Phineas!" I look up and see Malchus and Eleazar enter the compound. They're both grinning and Malchus waves a crumpled piece of parchment in his hand. "A letter," says Malchus, "from Marta, my loved one."

"My sister," Eleazar adds.

"What does she write?"

"I won't read everything," he says, and blushes slightly, "but she says that the rumours are true. Their cousin went to the capital and met with others from The Way. They really did nail him and he died, but now the tomb is empty and many of The Way have seen him alive. He's not a ghost – they've eaten with him." Malchus looks up, his eyes shining. "Phineas, he's alive!"

"We should go to the capital," I say. I don't care about the pain travel will cause me. "Let's meet with him ourselves."

Malchus shakes his head. "No, it's still too dangerous. Marta writes that the teacher has told everyone to wait because he is sending them a gift."

"A gift?" I'm intrigued. "We don't want to miss out. We should definitely go to the capital."

"We should wait," says Malchus. "When he comes back here, we'll be ready for him."

"Yes," says Eleazar slowly. "We should be ready for him." We can tell he's thinking about something. "How many people did he cure here in this town?" He doesn't wait for an answer. "There must be many others like you, Malchus, who believe the message of the teacher. Why don't we gather them together and let them know what's happened? We can teach them and tell them more about the teacher's words."

"We're meant to be keeping a low profile," says Malchus.

"If the teacher could save me from death once, he can save me again," Eleazar replies defiantly, and I notice a stubbornness in him that reminds me of me.

So, that's what Eleazar does. He doesn't go shouting in the market, but he does search out people who he's heard were cured by the Master. There's one older woman he introduces to me. She doesn't speak my language, so Malchus translates, but it turns out that she too was tormented by spirits. They would seize her and she wouldn't remember what happened at that moment but afterwards would wake up injured or sometimes in jail. The Master set her free, and she decides to join our meetings. Her name is Maryam. We call her Auntie Maryam because there's a young girl, also called Maryam, who had a skin disease. It wasn't leprosy but she would scratch herself until she bled. The teacher cured her as well and she also joins us.

Then there are a few fishermen who would normally be sleeping in the afternoon but who follow The Way. Also a woman who had a deformed hand that the Master grew back and another young girl who had a hunchback. She doesn't now, and I can't help noticing how pretty she is. We meet around the shaded platform in Malchus's compound garden during the afternoon while his family are inside sleeping. The women usually bring their children and some of them invite their relatives or neighbours to join us. Soon there's not enough room for us all to sit together and we sprawl out, sitting under the nearest trees for shade.

I'm the only one who doesn't speak their language so Malchus sits next to me and translates. When he's teaching, there's another young man who is a childhood friend of Malchus, called Rufus, and he translates.

I've stayed too long to be a guest, so each morning I get up early with Pappus and his wife and help smoke the previous night's catch of fish. My wound heals nicely and I'm able to help just as much as anyone else, if not more. I don't want to be a burden on this family. I start going with Pappus down to the lake each morning to collect the fish, as I find I miss daily contact with the water. I also go swimming after our afternoon talks as the sun sets. I swim alone and I remember my friend Nicanor. I pray for him and for Rabba and Demarchia. I want them to meet the Master one day.

I learn a lot about the Master and his teachings. Some of the simplest things he teaches are the hardest things to actually put into practice. The Master says that if someone swindles you out of your cloak, you should also give them your tunic. I've never heard such a thing. Or, if someone punches you on the right side of your face, offer them your left side as well. I don't know anyone who can do that. Eleazar is pretty good at trying to answer our questions but says when he doesn't know the answer. This still happens quite a bit and just makes me even more impatient to travel down to the capital and meet the Master face-to-face.

However, as I learn more about the Master I discover just how often he came through this town, so he's sure to be back this way soon. There's so much I want to ask him. I realize that I don't really have any other plan for my life. All I want is to spend time with him and learn from him. Actually, there are three things I'd like to ask him for: the first, would be to forgive me for the things I've done that I can't undo. I think that's the most important. Then I'd ask him to visit my village. They only know him as the destroyer of pigs, but if he cured their sick and helped people; if my family could just meet him…

The third thing I'd ask is if he can cure me of the nightmares I have every night. I woke up one morning with my hand around Pappus's throat. He accepted my apology but had bruise marks for the next few days and has learned to wake me with caution. The spirits don't inhabit my days, but they still inhabit my nights.

The weather gets warmer and I barely need a sheet to sleep under at night. Then we get more news from the capital and it's not what I want to hear at all. One of the Master's followers has written a short letter to Malchus. Malchus reads it out to all of us at our afternoon gathering. Rufus translates for me. The note says that the Master has gone but isn't dead. They watched him taken up into the sky, higher and higher until he was gone. The note tells us that everyone is now waiting for the gift but no one knows what it will be.

"How long will he be up there for?" I ask, realizing that it doesn't even seem that strange after everything else I've learned about him. "When will he come back down again?"

"I don't know," says Malchus. "The letter doesn't say more. We just have to wait for this gift he talked about."

I wait until that evening when it's just the three of us lying together and looking up at the stars. "You said that we should wait for the Master to come and visit us. Now you say he's gone. Does that mean we've missed our chance?"

"He's done what he came to do and now he's gone back to the Father," says Eleazar.

"But he hasn't done what he came to do, El," I say, sitting up and trying not to let my voice crack. "I needed to see him again and now he's gone. I thought he could make me free. I mean, really free of the nightmares and the things I did. Why didn't he come here? Why has he abandoned us?"

"Why do you think I have all the answers?" Eleazar snaps. We're all silent in the dark. "Sorry," he adds, and then sighs. "I don't understand it either."

Malchus just puts an arm around me. I think that's probably the best answer he can give right now.

We still meet with the others every afternoon but my enthusiasm has gone. I feel let down and angry. What am I supposed to do now? I've put all my fish on one tray and now it's been taken away from me. My life just seems aimless.

One afternoon, instead of joining the others at our gathering, I take a few coins from my pouch and head to the baths. At first it's relaxing and enjoyable to sweat and then to shave my patchy beard. After scraping the oil off I wander into the courtyard and go over to the wrestling and running. The young men are mostly uncircumcised, and they glance down at me and move away, knowing the laws about not getting too close. I want to reassure them that I'm not like the others, but is it true? Where do I fit now? I feel lost.

I leave the baths having spoken to no one and am heading back towards the compound, but I don't think I can face the gathering in my current mood. So instead I go to the lake for a swim, even though I've just got clean at the baths. Swimming always makes me feel better, although in this case I find myself just missing Nicanor more. Back on shore, I stand letting the afternoon sun dry me, and I find myself praying, asking what I'm supposed to do with my life. Why am I here? Where do I belong? How can I be free from the past or make it right in some way?

I don't get an answer and return to the compound. I'm still on the street when I hear a commotion from inside. Have the religious authorities found Eleazar? I hurry forward and burst through the door.

There's someone I don't recognize. He's placing his hands on people and praying for them and then they start weeping or laughing or both and then they praise God. I know they're praising God because Aunt Maryam, who doesn't speak my language, is weeping and praising him fluently in my tongue without even a trace of an accent. How is this possible?

I see Eleazar bowed over, weeping. I put my hand on him.

"Are you all right?" I ask.

He just hugs me. "It's the gift the teacher promised. It's come!"

"Where is it?" I ask, looking around.

"It's everywhere! The teacher is here. He *is* the gift! Now I understand what my sisters were talking about." He looks up at me, eyes wild with passion. "A jar of perfume must be broken for the fragrance to be released. Why couldn't I see it? He's everywhere now. He's in the capital and he's also here – right here," he gestures around wildly, "and here…" He puts his hand on his heart.

"I don't understand," I say, but then the man I don't know comes up to me, Malchus by his side.

"This is our brother Phineas," says Malchus in my language.

"Grace and peace to you, Phineas. I'm Filipus," he says. "Can I pray for you?"

I nod and he begins praying. I don't understand what he's saying, but I do know that this isn't the language of the north shore. "Brother Phineas," he says to me after a while. "He remembers you under the pomegranate tree." He looks up at me to see my response.

"What?" I say, trying to keep my voice even. My heart has begun to beat wildly and my palms are suddenly slick with sweat.

"He was there with you under the pomegranate tree," says Filipus again.

I feel a churning in my stomach as I see my hands smash Aqub's head against our courtyard flagstones and feel it break like a ripe pomegranate.

"He sees you. He knows what happened. He wants you to be free," says Filipus. I glance at Malchus, trying to remember what I've told him and what he might have told Filipus, but Malchus just looks confused.

"But I can never make it right. I can never fix it," I whisper.

"No, but he has," says Filipus, drawing closer and placing his hand gently on my head. "Let him fill you. Know his forgiveness and let it cleanse you, washing you clean inside."

My knees buckle. I've straddled Aqub and I'm beating his head, and then it isn't him any more; it's Timaeus, crying out in fear at what I'm about to do to him. Then he becomes a soldier between my legs, begging for mercy as I rip off his ear with my teeth. Other memories come too, of Berenice and Mother. I can't stop sobbing. "Help me," I manage to gasp. It's the only thing I can pray. They gather around me, each of the people I've hurt. I cower, trying to back away from them. Then I see the Master, standing between me and them. "I'm so sorry," I whimper.

He reaches down and takes me up in his arms. "I'm making you new," he says. And then I'm on fire.

I'm being burnt up, except this isn't painful. I feel as if my whole body is being scoured with light. I look down at my hands and I see the bonds that bind me to the past and to all the things I've done wrong. The Master breaks each one effortlessly and I feel awash with forgiveness. Then I watch as he places new bonds on my wrists. They shine like gold. There are no chains, just these flashing golden bands around my wrists. "We're all bound to something," he says, as I look up and our eyes meet. "Will you be bound to me?"

"Yes," I say, my voice trembling. "Let me be with you always."

"Always," he says, and I'm so overwhelmed at how little I deserve this second chance.

"Thank you," I whisper to him, and as the vision fades I find myself laughing and crying at the same time. I don't know how long I stay like this, but at some point I start to speak out words of praise. I don't know what I'm saying – I just know that these are words straight from my heart to God. I see Malchus's mother, and I feel such an urge to speak to her. I'm still shaking with emotion as I continue to praise God. Her eyes widen because I'm speaking to her in her own language, which she knows I don't know. Then she falls to her knees and she begins to weep. Filipus comes and places his hands on her head and that just makes the weeping worse, and it seems to last for a long time, but then she looks up. Her face is glowing and she begins to shout out praises in a way that seems undignified for a woman of her age, but so beautiful at the same time.

I turn back to Filipus. "Once I was filled with an army of spirits," I say quietly. "The Master rescued me from them but they still haunt my dreams, every night."

"Now he fills every part of you that was given to darkness," he says, placing his hand on my heart and again I feel the power and the light pass through me as easily as water through a fishing net.

I start crying again. Before, I was filled with spirits and I was strong. Then I was empty of spirits and I was weak. Now I have *his* spirit in me. All his power is in me, but it's not trying to control me, it's simply there. The guilt is gone, but so is the emptiness, and for the first time in my life I feel full inside.

Eventually I flop to the ground, exhausted. I watch as Malchus's mother calls her daughter-in-law and Pappus to her and tells them what is happening to her. Then she places her hands on them and prays. I don't know what she's saying, but I see the results. I watch as the Master's power passes from one person to the next, like a contagion. We waited for the Master to come and he has, but not like we thought he would.

Eventually the weeping and praising subsides a little and we hear Filipus raise his voice. "If you want to start a new life, come and let the old one die and be buried."

I don't really know what he means, but I know that I want to start a new life. So I'm one of the first to follow him out of the compound door. We head down to the lake. Filipus strips off his tunic and wades into the water up to his waist. "Drown your old lives and the old ways. Leave them here in the waters and come up cleansed, ready to start again," he calls out.

There's something so compelling about those words, and before I know it, I've stripped off my tunic and run into the water. "Let this water be like a grave to you," he says. "As you come out of it, your old life dead, let your new life, filled with *him*, begin."

He plunges me under the water and holds me there for a while, and I remember Cephas and how he pulled me out of the waters when I tried to kill myself. I imagine dying right now and being re-born and think about what I want to leave behind. I don't have much time to think but just before he lifts me out of the water, I remember the vision I had of all those faces of people I've hurt, and I know that I want to leave that behind in the water and start a new life. As I come up gasping for air, and look around me at the joy-filled faces, as well as the curious who've gathered around us, I know what I want to do with my life. If there's one thing I want, it's to see my brother and my mother again; to try to seek their forgiveness for all I've done to them, and to tell them about the Master. I realize that while the Master could even break the bonds that bound me to the terrible things I'd done, there were some bonds he didn't break. The bond that anchors me to my family is still there, and I don't think it can ever be broken. However dangerous, I know that I have to take this precious gift of the Master's spirit and go back to them.

Chapter Fifteen

I feel his hand gently shaking me awake. It's quiet all around us. "Hello," he says quietly, with a big grin on his face. I don't know what's so funny and rub sleep from my eyes. "Thanks for not trying to kill me," he adds.

It takes me a further moment to realize. "The nightmares, they're gone," I whisper.

He just keeps grinning back. "You have *his* spirit living in you now," he says.

I yawn and stretch. "I can't remember the last time I slept so well," I say. "Do you still feel different?" He nods. "Me too." We sit in silence for a while. Filipus and Eleazar are still asleep on mats beside us. "What did your father say?"

He'd been at a wedding and came home late to find that everyone in his household is now a follower of the Master. I'm not sure he's very happy about it.

"He didn't say much and nor will I," says Malchus. "I'm going to let Pappus and Mother do the talking. Let them tell him about what happened and how they have the Master's gift in them now."

"Malchus," I say, and then pause as I try to find the right words. His face becomes serious as he can tell I've got something important to say. "I think it's time for me to leave. You've taught me so much about the Master, and Filipus brought the Master's gift to us. Now I need to go back to my village and take the gift to them as well. He told me to tell my family and my village about the goodness of God and I still haven't done that."

"But you told me it was too dangerous for you to go back there," he says. "And there's so much more you can learn from Filipus now that he's here."

"You're right, and maybe I'll stay another day or so, but then I've got to go back, even if it's dangerous. Remember what Eleazar said? If the Master could bring him to life once, he can do it again. I don't want to be afraid of being afraid any more."

Malchus nods and looks up, eyes glassy with tears. "We're really going to miss you," he says.

I smile. "But you won't be here for long, will you? What about this fiancée of yours?"

"Yes, it's about time we headed back to her village. First, I want my family to learn more about the teacher. A week with Filipus and Eleazar should give them a good start."

"You can come and visit me," I say. "We'll let you stay even if you are circumcised." Malchus smiles. There's a knock at the compound door.

"I hope you don't mind us turning up so early," says a young girl whose name I forget, but I've seen her at the last few afternoon gatherings. "Is Brother Filipus awake?" She enters shyly. "I brought my sisters," she says in my language. Their family is mixed; her father is like me, and her mother is one of them. She introduces the two sisters and Malchus lays down a seating mat in the shade of one of the fig trees. I nudge Eleazar and Filipus awake. "When I came home yesterday, they didn't even know about the gift, but they could see that I was different," the girl explains. "Salome said I was glowing." She smiles shyly as Salome nods. "And I told them about the gift and how your mother was filled with the gift as well, and Salome gets these terrible headaches, and we were hoping…"

Malchus glances over at Filipus, who is shuffling bare feet into sandals and seems about to head to the latrine. Filipus looks up, bleary-eyed. "Malchus, you know he called it a gift for a reason," he says, his voice still gravelly with sleep. "It's not only mine to give. You can pray for the girls too. I'll join you soon." He rubs a knot in his shoulder and heads for the latrine.

By the time he's finished there and splashed water on his face, we've joined the young girl, placing our hands on the heads of Salome and her other sister and asking the spirit of the Master to pour into them. Malchus prays for the power of the Master to stop the headaches and the girl, Salome, weeps, falling to her knees as her sobs turn to wails. We keep praying and another hand joins ours. It's Filipus, and then Eleazar joins us and then Malchus's mother comes and prays over the girls as well. Soon wails turn to gasps of joy and the girls begin to call out praises to God. It truly is amazing.

There's another knock on the door and Malchus answers it. A bearded face peers around him at us and relaxes. "I just didn't want to wait until this afternoon," he says. "I'm not the only one?"

It's like this all day. People keep dropping by, often bringing friends, neighbours or relatives to join us. The story is usually the same: a hunger to experience the Master's gift again and a desire to tell others about him. Eleazar translates for me what one of the young boys is saying. "This is my father. He holds an important seat in our prayer house and he's always been against the teacher and tried to stop me visiting you. But last night, when I came home, I couldn't stop praising God and he could see that I'd changed." The father, a tall, gaunt man with a long beard, nods. He looks uncomfortable, but there's also an eagerness in his eyes. Salome, the girl who had headaches before, comes up to him. "Uncle," she says respectfully, but with authority that belies her age, "receive the sacred spirit of the teacher." He kneels before her and she places her hands on his head and soon he's doubled over, wiping streaming eyes on the hem of his robe as he weeps with such deep emotion.

Filipus told us last night that when the gift came to them in the capital, it was like wind and fire resting on the heads of everyone. I think I understand. This gift is like the wind, blowing through our lives like a storm and leaving us changed forever. It's also contagious, like fire, keen to burn wherever there's fuel for it.

"Will you pray for me again?" I ask Eleazar. He places a hand on my head and the gift comes. If gratitude was water, I'd be drowning right now. I start crying and thanking the Master, this time in my own language. I thank him for being like the broken jar of perfume, releasing this gift so that anyone anywhere can feel it pouring over them, into them, through them.

I look up as a young, clean-shaven man with tightly curled hair comes through the door guiding a short, tense woman who looks around her with suspicion. His other arm rests on the shoulder of a younger, leaner, darker version of himself, who must be his brother. Beside him is a beautiful young woman who holds her swollen belly in one hand, her other hand held by a girl barely old enough to walk. I watch as they fall down on their knees together and it seems as if light, fire and water dance all around them, washing darkness off them. They begin to laugh and weep and hug each other. I blink and they're gone. It seemed so real: my family filled with the Master's sacred spirit. I can't stop weeping and shouting, "May it be as I've seen, Master." I long for my family so much.

By midday our group is too large to be seated comfortably and the young perch on tree branches and the compound walls. We listen as Filipus teaches us more about the Master. Eventually he glances at the noonday sun and we stop. Everyone hurries home, or to the market if their home is too far away, returning with baskets of food which we share together. Then Filipus tells us more.

The sun has set, leaving a warm afterglow, by the time we disperse. I turn to Malchus and tell him about my vision. "I know I won't find any fishing boats going to my village from here, but I'm going to see if one of the boats can drop me off in that direction. I can't delay any longer." He nods sadly. "You've been like a brother to me. Thank you for doing all you could to let me stay with you."

Malchus grabs me and hugs me tight and I hear his weeping in my ear. "You have taught me so much," he whispers. "You challenged us and you were right. This gift is for everyone."

Malchus calls the remnants of our group together, along with his family, and tells them about my plan to return to my village. "What Phin plans to do is dangerous," Malchus explains. "For all we know, the villagers will take him straight outside the village and stone him. Let's pray for the Master to lead and guide him and keep him safe."

After they've prayed I embrace each of the men and thank Malchus's mother and sister-in-law and Pappus for their hospitality. They've never asked me for money and even though I worked hard while I was here, they've been generous to have me.

"You taught me more than you know," says Eleazar quietly as we embrace. "Just remember, if he wants to, he can bring you back from the dead."

Malchus and Eleazar walk with me down to the shore and help haggle with some of the fishermen, who all know Malchus from the fish-smoking. One of the boats will be tacking along the shoreline heading south-west, and they agree to take me on board and accept just one coin for their troubles. We embrace one last time, and this time we all weep. "Pray for my village," I say. "And especially for my brother, Timaeus."

I strip off and attract a few curious looks from the fishermen, who see that I'm circumcised but also realize I can't speak their language. I bundle my clothes into my satchel and carry it with my sandals over my head, wading up to my shoulders and then climbing into the waiting boat.

I wedge myself into a space up in the prow of the boat and with the rocking motion and fresh night air I'm soon asleep, waking only when a fish flops frantically against my ankle. I look around and see that although it's still dark, the moon is hanging heavy in the sky and dawn isn't far off.

"Get ready," says one of the fishermen, and I can hear waves breaking not far from us. "This is as far as we go," he says.

I strip again. "Are you sure it's shallow enough here?" I ask. He nods and I hand him my bundle of clothing and then vault over the side, gasping at the cold. I'm up to my neck and the fisherman passes me my bundle and wishes me a good journey. I wade to the bay and stand, teeth chattering, trying to dry off a little before I put my tunic and cloak on. I see some trees nearby and wrap myself in my cloak, use the satchel as a pillow, and fall asleep under them.

I'm woken by the sun. The bay is deserted but there is a path leading up from it. I relieve myself behind some rocks, go for a brief swim to wake me up properly, and then head up the path. It joins the main road, which I follow south. I'm one step closer to my village.

I walk for several hours and the road climbs into the hills. Then I come to a fork in the road that leads down to a large town spread out along the lake shore. I think I know where I am. This was where Nicanor and Rabba hoped to continue their journey. I pray for them and stop at a small stall in the shade of a tree beside a spring. I fill up my water-skin and buy some boiled eggs and flatbread. The old woman picks a tree leaf and spoons a clump of moist salt into its centre, wrapping it for me to dip my eggs into.

I don't rest for long as I want to get as far as possible before noon. I pass a camel caravan and several trains of donkeys heading in the opposite direction, and ask how long it will take to get to my village. One tells me tomorrow morning and the other tomorrow evening. Either way, I won't arrive today. I wear the prayer shawl to keep the sun off my head as I continue past noon, looking for a good spot to stop and rest. I see a cluster of trees ahead which looks promising, but then hear a youth calling out to me for help.

I've been told about thieves who prey on the kindness and gullibility of strangers. For all I know, the man lying down in the shade beside the youth is about to leap up and place a knife at my throat. I approach warily. "I'm supposed to be looking after him," says the youth, his voice trembling. "He was already sweating, even before we left, and told me I had to get him to a decent doctor in the main town. He's too large to ride my donkey and by the time we reached here he couldn't walk any more. I don't know what to do."

I come closer and peer at the man. He's lighter skinned, with close-cropped hair, and looks foreign. Even though he only wears a waist cloth, his muscular, scarred body is shiny with sweat. Then I notice something that suddenly makes me recoil. "I'm sorry," I stammer. "I can't help you." I turn and I'm about to walk away, forcing myself not to run, but the boy grabs hold of my wrist.

"Please, don't leave me alone with him. Feel his forehead. He's burning up. I don't know what to do. What if he dies?"

"I can't help you. I need to go," I say, trying to keep the fear out of my voice.

"What am I going to do?" the boy wails, and starts to snivel.

"Look, the town isn't that far," I say. "I can help drape him over your donkey. If you have some rope we can tie him on."

"He's too sick to move," says the boy, and as if to confirm this, the sweating man starts coughing violently. "Please help me. What will his commander do if I arrive there with a dead body? You know what they're like."

I'm trapped and can't see how I can stay or how I can leave. I glance over at the man again to confirm what I already know. A chunk is missing from his left ear where it was bitten off. I did that. He's one of the soldiers who once came to arrest me. If he recognizes me, what then? I place a hand on his forehead. He's burning up and won't last long at this rate. "Do you have a water-skin?" I ask and the boy nods, scrabbling for it in his saddlebags. I take off my prayer shawl and soak it, using it to mop the soldier's brow. I don't think it's helping much.

I do this for a while and then the soldier moans and arches his back. I think he's convulsing.

"Do something," says the boy, whom I glance at resentfully. When did this become my problem?

I place a hand on the soldier's brow and I pray aloud. I ask the Master to cure him with his power. I pray that this soldier would experience the Master's power and would want to follow the Master. I close my eyes, crying out. When I open them the soldier is completely still except for his eyes, which look up at me. "What are you doing?" he croaks with a thick accent.

"The gods be praised," says the boy. "We thought you were going to die."

"I... I'm praying for you. I didn't know what else to do. You have a very bad fever." I reach down and feel his forehead again. It feels cool. I laugh. "You *had* a very bad fever. Now you don't. It was him – he cured you."

"Who?" The soldier swivels his eyes around.

"The Master, the one everyone is talking about. They tried to kill him in the capital, but they couldn't keep him dead. He's the one who cured you. He's given us his power."

"All I know is that a week ago Max died of the same fever I had. I wasn't even sure I'd make it to the town." He fixes his eyes on me. "I owe you my life," he says.

I help the soldier sit up and offer him a sip of the water-skin. He downs the lot greedily and then belches. Then he gets up and flexes his shoulders, rotates his neck and shakes out his limbs, laughing a little. "I'm all right," he says, looking at the boy.

He lifts his waist cloth and urinates. We avert our eyes. We would go behind a rock or a tree. "So," he says as he pees, "who is this Master you're talking about?"

I should tell him. I should tell him everything, but what if he tries to arrest me? He still doesn't recognize me and there's no reason why he should. "I would love to tell you more," I say, "but I've got to be on my way. I'm going in the opposite direction." I point south.

"Then you can tell me on the road," he says, clapping a hand on my shoulder. "We've no reason to head into town any more."

The boy untethers his donkey and the soldier brushes dried grass from the robe he was lying on, and then we leave. I tell him about the Master, mainly telling him the things I've heard from Malchus and Eleazar. Of course, he's heard about the Master, too.

"What's this have to do with me?" he says, after listening for a while. "This man's one of the cock-cutters. You know what they're like with foreigners."

"Yes, yes I do," I say. "But he didn't just come for them. He came for everyone."

"How do you know?" he asks, and then, before my better judgment can get the better of me, I tell him about my childhood and about Aqub and then about how I ended up being controlled by the spirits. The boy listens too and neither of them interrupts much. Who doesn't like a good story on a long journey? Then I get to the bit about living in the cave among the dead.

I see recognition flicker then kindle in his eyes. "It was you, wasn't it?" he says, stopping and turning to face me. "You did this." He grabs the blunt edges of his bitten ear.

"It was the spirits in me who –"

I don't finish because he's grabbed me by the throat and thrown me to the ground. I'm choking and scrabbling in the dust but his grip is too tight. I can't breathe and my vision begins to grow dark. The boy jumps on him, trying to tear him off me, but the soldier just flings him aside. I think what might be my last thought, which is that I'm really sad not to see my family again. Then suddenly he lets go and I gulp down as much air as I can. I skitter away from him on my back, but he doesn't chase after me. He's just sitting there, puzzled.

"I swore on more gods than I can remember that I would find you and kill you," he says quietly. "And now I can't. This has never happened to me before."

I slow my panting down and try to speak, but all I can do is cough. "I didn't want this," I finally manage to wheeze. "You've heard what they did to me. Do you know how many times I tried to kill myself to get away from those spirits? I was their prisoner. I never meant to hurt anyone."

He looks at me, fingering his torn ear, and then punches the ground hard with his fist. If that had been my face, it would have broken my cheekbone.

"You said that you owed me your life," I say warily. "But I think I owed you. Look at me. I'm no match for you in a fight, but remember what I did to your whole section? How could I have done that if not for the spirits?" He still breathes heavily and looks as if he might lunge for me. "I'm sorry," I add quietly, and then I pull off my tunic and let him see the scars on my chest. "If it makes you feel any better, you're not the only one who got hurt."

He stands up and walks over to me. I brace myself for pain, but instead he offers me a hand up. "You've paid your debt," he says gruffly. He turns to the boy and beckons him to follow.

"My father gave money to the young men in our village who went hunting for you," says the boy. "Our village had pigs in that herd too. We lost all our savings and my sister's marriage got delayed by a year. You're crazy to be heading back in this direction. If anyone finds out who you are, they'll kill you."

"Not if he's with me," says the soldier, and we walk on.

By sunset we arrive at the fork in the road that leads off to their village. We've spent most of the way talking about the Master. The boy offers for me to stay in his house. I thank him, but I don't think it's safe for me to do that. He tells us to wait and trots off on his donkey in a cloud of dust. We sit beside the road, and I ask the soldier what he misses most from home. By the time the boy returns, we have talked about foreign girls and food and are just getting on to the arena and games. The boy takes out a large flatbread folded in half. It's filled with goat's cheese, olives, a couple of dried sardines and slices of cucumber. He stuffs it into my satchel and then it's time for us to part ways.

"It's not too late for you to turn back," says the soldier. "I'm telling you, tactically, as a soldier, this won't end well. Not with the enemies you've made."

I don't deny it. "I have to see my family again," I explain. "I have to tell them about the Master. It's as simple as that."

The soldier claps me on the shoulder and then turns with the boy and they take the path towards their village. I sit down and eat the boy's food. Maybe I am being reckless, I reason, but then the soldier and the boy both had good reason to turn me in, beat me up or even kill me, and yet I'm still breathing.

I decide to press on in the near-dark, the sky the colour of bruises, hoping to avoid our neighbouring village, which also lost huge numbers of pigs, and see if I can reach my village before dawn.

The moon rises and, although I'm tired, I also feel tense with anticipation as I start to recognize landmarks. I keep walking as the path gets higher and then see, down to my left, the slopes off which the pigs cascaded. Below them are the caves of the dead. The quickest way back to my house would be to take the little path that leads down to those caves. I feel a queasiness in my stomach but steel myself and begin the trudge down. The path is horribly familiar.

This is where the spirits would drive me during storms. I remember my teeth biting down on the squealing pig in my hands, feeling it writhing in pain and terror. Part of me wonders why I want to be here alone with the horrors of the past, but I think I need this. It's good to remember the bad, so I can also remember what the Master did for me; how he saved me from it all.

I pick my way down to the caves and find the one I lived in. This is where I tried to rape my brother; where I hurled obscenities at my mother and tore the garment she made me. Although I never broke their bones or bit off their ears, I hurt them much more deeply than any of those soldiers.

The ratty old blanket I used to curl up in is gone. In fact, there's nothing in the cave to indicate that I ever lived there. Nicanor once told me how the Master made enough food out of one person's lunch to feed thousands. Can he take whatever is good in me and somehow multiply it to make up for all the bad things I've done? I wrap myself up in my cloak and prayer shawl and lean back against the stone wall of the cave, closing my eyes for a moment as I think about what to do next.

I wake the next morning and the sun is already high. I sit up and try to work out what my next move should be. If I go straight home during daylight I might be recognized along the way. Do I wait in the cave for nightfall? That seems a better option, but by then Timaeus will be out on the lake and he's the one I yearn to see most. I'm not sure what to do. I sit at the mouth of the cave, staring out at that familiar view of the lake until the sun is too hot and I retreat into the shadows. I'd forgotten just how hot our village gets. In the village, anyone who can will retreat into the cool interior of their home to sleep through the heat of the day, which means that the streets should be pretty deserted. I scan the path to the village and it's empty. So I collect my things and start towards it.

As I get nearer I can see heat shimmering off the flat roofs. I glance up at Berenice's house. I suppose I shouldn't think of it as that any more as our house is now her home. I wonder if Antigona has finally started speaking to her daughter again, or if she has at least acknowledged her own granddaughter. Surely she can't hold a grudge that long? How will it be for me when I see Timaeus and Berenice together? Will they find it awkward as well? That's assuming I get to see them. I don't even know if my mother will let me into the courtyard.

I walk down our street. A door opens and I freeze. A young girl I don't recognize comes out with a bucket of dirty water which she sluices over the cobbles. She doesn't look up and I'm glad I haven't tried to hide myself under the prayer shawl, as I think that might draw more attention. I arrive at our door and I'm about to knock but then I try it to see if it's open, and it is. I slide inside, closing it quietly behind me. The courtyard still looks more or less the same and smells of the drying fish that are festooned everywhere. I glance over at the pomegranate tree, wondering if I'll experience that same sickening feeling as I remember what happened under it. I don't. I feel sad that I did it, but the weight of guilt is gone now.

I go to the inner door of our house and knock gently. My heart pounds and my hands are clammy with sweat. The door opens.

Chapter Sixteen

Berenice opens the door groggily, squinting in the sunlight. Her belly is swollen, just like in my vision. It takes her a moment to register who I am and then her eyes widen.

"Hello, Berenice," I say, feeling really awkward. "It's me. Is... is my brother here?"

"Who is it?" I hear a voice from inside. It's Timaeus.

Berenice doesn't say anything. She just stands aside with the door open. I can see several sleeping mats on the floor. Timaeus sits up, his hair rumpled. He looks at me, shading his eyes, but I don't think he can see me properly because the sunlight is behind me.

"Phin?" It's my mother. She's still curled with her granddaughter spooned into her, but she looks up and knows me right away.

"It's good to see you again, Mother," I say.

Timaeus just stares at me as if I'm not real, his face puzzled.

"Can I come in?" I ask, directing my question at Tim. He's the head of the household now.

Timaeus looks to his mother and then at Berenice; all that passes between them is uncertainty. "Why are you here?" he asks.

"I don't know if it's safe for me to come back," I answer. It isn't really an answer. "I just couldn't wait any longer. I had to see you all again. I've missed you so much. And there's something important I have to tell you."

There's a silence that seems to go on forever. In the end it's Berenice who breaks it. "Well, get up then," she says to Timaeus. "Let's make some room."

Suddenly everyone is busy putting away bedding and laying out seating mats and placing a food cloth on the floor which they cover with flatbread, bowls of olives, dried fish, and raisins. I'm given a seat while they move around me. I suppose it's just showing the usual courtesy to a guest, but I don't want to feel like a guest, like a stranger in my own home. I glance over at the alcove and see that the statue I smashed on Aqub's head has been replaced with more statues. The little girl toddles over to me and looks up with big, dark eyes. She's beautiful. I take her little hands in mine and say, "What's your name?" in that voice you're supposed to use with small children.

She understands and puts a hand on her chest, but she can't speak yet.

"It's Verutia," says Berenice, as she layers the bedding away.

"That's your grandmother's name, too," I say. She nods and looks over at Mother, who is watching me. They're all watching me out of the corners of their eyes, wary and still uncertain. There's a horrible formality about the way I'm seated and offered food and a bowl of hot mint tea, like they would if I was Aqub. They sit clustered together and I'm seated slightly apart. The only family member who's even touched me is my niece Verutia. I suppose it's good that Berenice didn't scramble to scoop her up and keep her away from me. I think they can see that I'm not the monster they knew any more.

"This tea is so refreshing," I say, desperate to fill the silence. Really, it's just tea. "Thank you," I add. Then there's more silence. I used to love the companionable quiet I had with Nicanor, but this feels horrible. "Oh, I have something for you," I say, and rummage around in my satchel, pulling out the pouch of coins. "It's from my wages over the past year. I tried to save as much as I could. I should probably give some of the coins to Tehinah to repay him for the cloak he gave me. He was very kind." I smile, but it slowly withers in the silence. "Here…" I pass it over to Timaeus. He doesn't take it, so I just set the pouch down on the food cloth beside him.

"How will a few coins help?" he asks. A muscle in his jaw pulses, and I can see that he's trying hard to contain his emotion. "If that whole satchel was filled with gold coins, do you think it would repair the damage you've done to our village, or the other villages around here?"

His question hangs in the air.

"No, I know it's not enough –"

"You can't just turn up here and think you can buy your way back. What are you even doing here, Phin? If Justus knew you were here he'd come over and gut you like a pig. You put us all in danger."

"So, should I just go then?" I say. My voice is raised. The resounding silence is an answer in itself. "Please, Timaeus," I say, my voice husky with emotion. "Whatever has happened between us, I'm still your brother. Surely that means something to you?"

Again, more silence.

"What's changed? You're still a hunted man. I don't understand why you came back," says my mother eventually.

"Because you're still my family. I'm still your son. I'm still your brother." I annoy myself by crying. I should probably just leave now and spare them any more trouble. This was not what I saw in my vision. But thinking about the vision reminds me of the Master and I pause for a moment, wiping my eyes on my sleeve. Little Verutia comes over to me, looking solemn, and wipes my cheeks. I smile and then I fold her into my lap. No one protests. I take a moment to recover my composure and offer up a quick prayer. Perhaps a little silence is good, given how badly my attempts at communication are going. Then I look up.

"I'm sorry I put you in this situation," I say. "You're right. It was foolish of me to come back. I came because I love you, but maybe I've hurt you too much for you to ever love me back. I will leave, but just let me say what I need to say." I see the tension in their bodies relax a little. This is good news for them. "Just a couple of hours. That's all I ask." There's an exchange of looks, but it's clear that they're all happy with this arrangement – although "happy" might be overstating it. They sit back to listen. I help myself to a handful of raisins and then I begin.

"You, the three of you, were the most important people in my life. I loved each of you so much. If you had been the only people in my life I would have been happy, but there was also Aqub. I will never forget the different ways he would hurt us. He was a blight on this household."

That's where I start my story. I don't mention everything. I don't know if Mother knows about some of the shameful things Aqub tried to do to me and Tim at night up on the roof. I remind them of that particular day that started so well, when Rufus asked me to join his boat. I try to hold their gaze, willing them to remember who I was before everything went wrong, hoping I can revive those old memories. When I recount that evening when we had to flee from our house, Berenice leans forward, interested. She probably hasn't heard the story in detail, or at least not my version. I don't know if Timaeus knows much about what actually happened either, so I tell them about the Teller and the incantations and the spirits entering me. I don't say anything about how Mother paid the Teller.

From this point on, Mother has tears streaming down her face. She's not sobbing; it's just as if her eyes have a leak. I tell them how the spirits gave me power and took away my fear. They really did protect me, but not in the way any of us would have wanted. I'm honest about how my own hatred for Aqub fuelled his murder. I don't blame the donkey and nor can I blame it all on the spirits.

I tell them about those first few days in the cave as the spirits set about imprisoning me in my own body. I remind them of each attempt they made to rescue me. "You knew it was dangerous. You knew that I wasn't myself any more, but you still tried. It was like you could see me down at the bottom of a well and you reached out as far as you could, but it was just too deep." I remind them how courageous and persistent they were in the midst of the horror of me being taken over and possessed by the spirits.

"There are things I did to you that I'd rather forget. Things I'd love to convince myself were just terrible nightmares and not real at all." Timaeus sits ashen-faced as I continue. I swallow, knowing this has to be done, and then speak of my attempt to dishonour my brother in the worst way possible; to hurt him so deeply that he would never come back again. I explain that it was the spirits who were in control, but that a part of me wanted to hurt Timaeus so that he would leave me alone in my shame. "Never have I been so grateful for someone cracking a stone against my skull," I say to Timaeus, smiling through my tears. "I don't deserve to be called your brother, but I want you to know that I have never stopped loving you and feeling proud of you, and I'm so grateful for this moment to ask you – to beg you – to find it in your heart to forgive me." He buries his face in his hands. My mother clutches her stomach as if in pain, but says nothing.

"And you," I say, turning to her. "You came to me, risked your life so many times, trying to bring me back. I remember the awful abuse I heaped on you, my own mother." I can't help but sob at this point, and then my mother comes forward.

"But you were still my son," she says, stroking my cheek. "I knew you were still in there somewhere."

I can't stop crying now. "I put you through hell," I manage to get out through the sobs. "I put you all through hell."

"It wasn't your fault," says my mother, putting an arm around me and running her fingers through my hair. Her touch just makes me cry more as I bury my head in her shoulder. "The fault was mine. It's always been mine. I could have called on Tehinah and the elders to do something about that dog Aqub. I could have gone to Tehinah that night instead of taking you to the Teller. I could have asked him to finally pay his debt."

I don't know what she means and I'm about to ask, but she begins to weep and instead I find myself consoling her. "I could never wish for another mother. You did everything you could."

"But look where it ended," Mother wails.

"It hasn't ended yet," I say, glancing up and smiling at Berenice and Timaeus through my tears.

I continue my story. My mother leans against me as I explain how many times I tried to kill myself. I show them my scars. I tell them about the time I ate poisoned food. I don't look at Timaeus because I don't feel any accusation towards him. I'm glad he tried to kill me and rescue me from that living hell.

Then I tell them about the Master and what happened with the pigs. I explain how the Master had power over the spirits. They knew who he was; they even knew his name. He was the one who freed me and sent the spirits into the pigs.

"Was that to punish our village?" says Timaeus. "What had we done wrong?"

"I'm not sure why he sent the spirits into the pigs, or what he would have done if the herd wasn't there. All I know is that he crossed a lake and came through a storm for me. Somehow he heard my cry."

I don't dwell on that first time I saw Mother and she told me to leave. I mention how kind Tehinah was, particularly as I'd broken his nose. Then I tell them about starting a new life as a tanner in the City of Horses and everything that happened to bring me back to this point. "And so I've brought something to you which is much more valuable than a whole satchel of coins. I want you to receive the Master's gift and see how he can break any chain and free us from anything that we're still bound to. How could I keep this to myself and not share it with the people I will always love most?"

I pause and sip the bowl of tea. I'm not used to speaking so much, but I think it's the Master's gift working in me, giving me the right words to say. We're all quiet for a moment, but it's not the same awkward silence as before.

"Now you've listened to me, I want to listen to you," I say.

"It's not been easy for us," says Berenice. "My brother started drinking after you left. And little Verutia doesn't even know him or her grandmother." Verutia looks up when she hears her name spoken. "But it's probably been easier for me than for them," she continues, nodding at Mother and Timaeus. "Through all the difficult times, our anger has kept us strong. We've blamed you for everything. It was the easiest course. It felt good even; such a relief not to have to defend you when people curse at your name or swear vengeance. And it's easier to simply hate you and consider you dead to us." She sighs. "But now you're here, reminding us of who you are. How can I hate you now? You suffered, too. We've all suffered. We've all paid a high price." She looks up and holds my gaze and I know she's reminding me that what happened has cost me her. I will only ever have her as my sister-in-law, not my wife. I don't look away. I nod, and understanding passes between us.

I turn to Timaeus. "I've talked too much," I say. "What about you, Tim? I know you've suffered greatly."

Timaeus rubs a hand over his face. "I've spent too long thinking about the cost I've paid," he says. "It's eaten me up inside." He looks up at the doorway and we see the pink light of the setting sun. "I'm going to have to go to work soon," he says.

"Greet Rufus for me," I say, without even thinking about it.

Timaeus looks at me, puzzled. "Phin, you attacked him, remember? You burnt our stores. He must never know you were here."

I swallow. Somehow, for a moment, I thought everything would be all right and that I could stay. "If you want me to, I'll leave in the night and when you come back tomorrow morning I'll be gone."

Timaeus looks at me and says nothing.

"Is that what you want?" I ask.

"I don't know!" he snaps, and then sighs. "I don't know what I want."

"I'll leave," I say, "but please let me stay until things are right between us."

He gives me a searching look, and then a barely perceptible nod. Then he turns and starts filling a satchel with food and a skin of water to take down to the boat.

Timaeus slides out through the compound door, ensuring that no one can see past him inside. Mother rules out us sitting in the courtyard for an evening meal in case the neighbours hear my voice.

It's funny how quickly normality descends on our inner room as Berenice hands me a bowl of soup as if she's always been my sister-in-law and nothing more. Mother tears a large flatbread and distributes it among us, pointing at me and saying "Phin" to Verutia. She struggles to attempt an "F" sound and makes us laugh, so Berenice teaches her the word "Uncle", and Verutia points at me each time she says it because she can see how much it makes us all smile.

I ask after relatives and neighbours. At first both Mother and Berenice are tentative, picking around delayed weddings, or boats not bought because of the loss of pigs and savings, but I don't flinch, and soon they just tell me everything. I start to realize just how disruptive the pig-herd deaths have been to everyone.

Then Mother starts to ask about the temples in the City of Horses and I tell her what little I know about the horse god, and the conversation inevitably leads back to the Master. I tell them how the Master cured Malchus and even brought Eleazar back from the dead. It turns out that the village has also heard many of the rumours about him leaving the cave of the dead and roaming throughout the land alive. "We dismissed all of it," says Mother. "All our village knows is that this man brings destruction."

We talk into the night, Verutia curled up asleep with her head resting on my leg. I suggest that I sleep up on the roof. It's dark now and I can carry bedding up there silently without arousing suspicion. As I lie there, looking up at the stars, I feel a profound sense of peace and gratitude. Finally, I'm doing what the Master told me to do. My family are hearing about the goodness of God. Even if Timaeus isn't ready to forgive me yet, he hasn't thrown me out. I start praying, but at some point fall asleep.

The next morning, I'm woken by the sound of someone entering the courtyard. I keep low, not wanting to attract attention, and see Timaeus enter with a flat basket of redbellies on his head.

"Have you got a spare basket?" I ask, getting up and putting on my waist cloth.

He gives me a silencing look and I realize how stupid I'm being, not just speaking aloud in the courtyard, where neighbours might hear, but even thinking I could go down to the bay. I'm not a very good fugitive. I slope silently down the steps and take the flat basket from him. "Do you still keep everything in the same place?" I ask. He nods and then heads back down to the bay, while I open the storage room and find the bag of salt, buckets and knives. Tim must be exhausted after a night's fishing, but still makes several journeys up and down with baskets of fish. I wonder if he normally gets a boy to do the carrying, and if it's because of me being here that he has to carry the baskets himself. I work quickly and have already gutted and salted half of the first basket by the time he returns with a second.

"How was the catch?" I ask. He shrugs and says nothing but sits himself beside me and takes over the salting and stringing of the fish. I spot Berenice about to emerge from the inner room, but when she sees us working together, she goes back inside. I think she wants to give us some time alone.

Sitting beside my little brother, I fight a continual urge to drop the knife and grab him in a fierce embrace, promising that I'll always be there for him, that I'll never hurt him again and telling him that I love him. Instead, I pass him fish after fish, and tentatively, keeping my voice hushed, I ask about the crew. His answers are short – curt even – but he does answer; we are talking. He yawns and I'm about to offer to finish the job myself so he can get some sleep, but just being with him feels good, so I don't.

"Do you remember how we always used to race each other down to the bay?" I ask, and he smiles sadly. "Who do you think would win now?"

"I don't know about running," he says, "but there's a foreign soldier stationed here. He's been teaching me to wrestle. I got sick of being beaten up."

"I've ended up choking in the dust a few times at the hands of foreign soldiers," I say, ignoring the lump in my throat at the thought of my little brother having to protect himself. I feel one of his biceps. "I'm pretty sure you'd beat me."

"I'm pretty sure, too," he says with a shy grin and a quick muscle flex.

"Tim…" I swallow, but I can't help myself and the tears come. "I feel like a part of me has been dead all this time. I've missed you so much." I can barely finish. "I'm so sorry."

The knife clatters to the ground and we don't care about smearing salt or fish guts on each other. I take him in my arms, and I feel his hot tears splashing on them as mine splash on his.

"I kept trying to kill you in my heart, trying to forget you, trying to hate you," he whispers after a while. "I thought I could do it, but I couldn't."

"I'm so sorry," I cry.

"I know," he whispers back.

I take his face in my hands. His eyes are puffy and red. "I won't leave you again," I tell him. "I don't care what the risks are. I'm not going anywhere."

He's about to say something, but then Verutia interrupts us with a wooden bowl of dates, which she offers to us. "Not now, my flower," says Timaeus, wiping his eyes with a shoulder. "We need to finish hanging the fish first, and then get cleaned up."

We make quick work of the remaining fish and decide to hang them all in the courtyard rather than risk me going up on the roof and being seen.

"I wish we could go down to the bay and wash off properly," I say, as I pour a stream of water from a stone jar and Timaeus scrubs off as much fishiness as he can. Berenice returns with the empty offal bucket. I wonder which neighbour she gives the entrails to now that her mother has disowned her.

We sit quietly together in the shade of the vine and eat breakfast. Mother and Berenice serve us. "Get off me," says Timaeus, smiling, as I put my hand around his neck for the fifth or sixth time, drawing his head to mine so that our foreheads touch.

After breakfast we hold council to discuss what to do next. Timaeus is the most sceptical of any attempt I might make to get the village to hear my side of things and give me a second chance. "Anyway, even if the village is willing to give you a second chance, you know what will happen when the soldiers hear that you're back."

"I can't just leave. I won't."

"We could leave with you," says Mother quietly. "Make a new start somewhere. It's not impossible."

But as we consider this option, and I think about the cost of land in the larger towns or cities, we realize that this isn't feasible either. We're not getting anywhere and Timaeus looks as if he's about to collapse from exhaustion. Then Mother says, "Let me talk to Tehinah. He owes me a debt." We wait for her to explain more but she doesn't. So I'm left playing with Verutia in the courtyard while Timaeus sleeps inside, Berenice goes to the market and Mother tracks down our village elder.

"He'll help," says Mother when she returns to the courtyard. By now it's noon and almost too hot to sit outside. "He's worried about you staying here any longer, especially as we're so close to Justus. He'll come soon, when everyone is indoors asleep, and then you must go with him."

I nod. "I still don't understand why he's being so helpful, especially after all the problems I've created for him."

Mother avoids my gaze. "He will explain everything himself," she says, and then goes inside to prepare lunch. Berenice returns from the market with fresh eggs and fresh flat loaves topped with hyssop, thyme, sesame, and olive oil. We eat quietly in the shade of the vine, the heat already shimmering over our flat roof. Then we slump, dozing in the shade until there's a quiet rap at the door. It's Tehinah.

Chapter Seventeen

Tehinah greets us, treating me with a distant formality. He carries a bulging cloth bag which he opens, pulling out the summer uniform worn by foreign soldiers. It doesn't include armour or a helmet, but these aren't always worn when soldiers are stationed at small villages like ours.

"Put it on," he says, "and I'll carry your clothes in this bag. I doubt there'll be many people on the street at this time of the afternoon but it's best to be safe."

I change and my hair is short enough that I might pass for a darker foreigner. "If all goes well, you'll see your family again later," he says.

"Should I wake Tim?" Berenice asks.

"No, let him sleep," I say. "God willing, I'll see him soon."

"Yes, gods willing," my mother adds, putting emphasis on the "s".

"We should go," says Tehinah. I step towards Berenice, and then I'm not sure if I should embrace her, and end up just patting her shoulder awkwardly. Not so Verutia, who runs at me and lets me sweep her up and give her a big kiss.

"I'm glad you've returned," says my mother quietly as she embraces me. "Forgive me," she whispers.

I'm about to tell her that I already have, but Tehinah interrupts. "Don't speak until we get back to my compound."

We leave, walking together at a brisk pace. As predicted, there's almost no one around until we get to the main square. Here, stalls are still set up, although most of the owners are slumped and snoring under the shade of hanging woven mats.

"Tehinah," one of the stallholders calls as we pass. I try not to tense. "I've been meaning to ask you about this new tax –" he starts, but Tehinah cuts him off.

"Not now. I have urgent matters to discuss with Felix here," he says, and turns before the stallholder bothers to scrutinize me. We walk to his compound gate and enter in.

I turn to Tehinah and smile. "That wasn't so difficult," I say.

"Come in," says Tehinah, motioning me towards his study. "It's all right. I've asked my wife to visit her sister this afternoon, so we won't be disturbed."

He leads me into a room with alcoves full of scrolls, a low rickety table with a lamp on it and some seating mats on the floor around it. We remove our sandals and kneel down on the mats. I take out the cloak. "Thank you for this," I say. "I wanted to return it to you."

"Is that why you came back?" he asks with a cocked eyebrow and a wry smile. "You're looking better than the last time we met." I want to say the same thing to him, but he doesn't look better. His tightly curled hair has greyed and thinned, and his face looks haggard and drawn. "So, here you are." He sighs. "Would you like something to eat?" he asks, jumping up. "I've forgotten my manners."

"No," I say. "No thanks, we've just eaten." There's something strange about his behaviour but I'm not sure what it is. It leaves me with a vague sense of unease. Tehinah seems disappointed, as if the busyness of preparing food would be better than us sitting down together and having to talk. "Your nose has healed up," I say.

He smiles ruefully. "Yes, a bit crooked, but my wife says it gives me character." He tails off, as if the mention of his wife has made him unhappy. Neither of us speaks for a moment, and then I break the silence.

"I owe you so much," I say. "And not just for the cloak or the others things you gave me. You could have called the nearest battalion and got me nailed. You've gone out of your way to help me." He gives a short, bitter laugh. I don't understand. "Tehinah, whatever the debt is that you owe my mother, you've more than paid it. I can never thank you enough. Is there anything I can do for you?"

Tehinah wipes away a tear. "I don't know how to tell you this," he whispers, refusing to meet my gaze.

"Tell me what?" I am so confused right now.

He gives a long sigh, as if resigning himself to the telling, and then gathers himself and begins. "As you know, I was once good friends with your father, Alpheus. We were the same age and got married the same year. Both of us were happy with our new wives at first, but then a year passed and neither wife became pregnant. There were the usual jokes in the beginning from our relatives about getting a move on, but then they were no longer jokes and the pressure grew. It put a strain on my marriage and on Alpheus and your mother. You know how it is with village gossip, and talk of us both marrying fruitless trees.

"Then one day your mother dropped by to visit my wife so they could commiserate together. But my wife was visiting her mother and I was at home alone. We…" He pauses, unwilling to meet my eye. "It just happened once. We never planned it, and afterwards we both felt terrible. We agreed that I would distance myself from Alpheus so that our paths wouldn't cross, and we would be kept apart. When I heard that Verutia was pregnant, and then saw how happy Alpheus was, I used this as an excuse to distance us from them, which wasn't hard as now it was just my wife who was barren and gossiped about. I hoped that the child was his. How could we know for sure who was the father, particularly as you take after your mother's side? When Timaeus was born, that gave me the reassurance I needed, that your father's seed was able to plant itself properly. Ever since, I've wondered if my wife is still barren as punishment from the gods for what I did."

He stops. I'm still trying to comprehend what he's saying.

"Can you see why I had to be careful not to involve myself with your mother and Aqub? I've always kept my distance and, as a result, you and Timaeus suffered under that man while I stood by and pretended it wasn't happening."

I remember how the spirits told my mother that they knew that Timaeus was only my half-brother. It never occurred to me that I might be the one with a different father.

"So, you're my father?" I ask.

Tehinah runs a hand through his beard. "We'll never know for sure, but…" he shrugs, "probably, yes."

I sit back, trying to take all this in. I feel numb.

"Did you and my mother ever talk about this? About me?"

He shakes his head. "I'm so sorry," he says quietly. "All of this mess… It all started with me. It's my doing."

There's a part of me right now that wants to get up and punch him. I want to shake him and ask him why he wasn't willing to claim me as his own, especially after my father – or whatever I should call Alpheus now – died. We could have avoided those years where Mother could barely feed us or, worse, when she took up with Aqub. The more I think about it, the more I want to smash his head against the paving stones like I did with Aqub.

I stop myself. How can I think like this after everything I've learned about the Master and after he's freed me from my past? I sit there in silence – Tehinah watching me – and try to get my thoughts straight.

Chris Aslan

"When I was here before, you saw that I was no longer a monster," I say slowly. "You shaved my head for me. You weren't afraid to touch me. You were the first person from our village to show me kindness. You helped me remember who I really was. I wanted to tell you something then." I pause and look up. Tehinah watches me, face pale and drawn. "I wanted to tell you what a good father I thought you'd make. But I didn't, because I realized this might not be very complimentary coming from a boy who bites other people's ears off." I've tried to make him smile but instead he dissolves into tears, drawing his knees up, hiding his face and sobbing into them. I come over to sit beside him, but he huddles away from me.

"No," he sobs.

I ignore this and put an arm around him. I'm surprised at myself. I think this is the Master's gift working in me again. "I forgive you," I say quietly, and then add, "Father."

This just makes him sob harder. I would never have thought Tehinah could cry like this and I even feel a little uncomfortable as I make shushing noises and pat the back of his neck. I notice just how tightly his hair curls; like mine.

Finally he gets up, wiping his cheeks with a sleeve. "Thank you," he says. "Just give me a moment." He goes outside and washes his face with water from a jar and then stands there, composing himself.

When he comes back in, I say, "After he freed me from the spirits, the Master told me to go back to my family and tell them about the goodness of God. I've already told my mother and Tim about what happened to me. Do you want to hear as well?"

Tehinah nods and sits back down.

I tell him everything. He asks me lots of questions about the Master, and smiles at my descriptions of Rabba and Demarchia. We pause for some water and dates. By the time I've told him about my family's reception of me, the sun is setting.

"My wife will be back soon," he says, "and we still haven't discussed what to do with you."

"I know it's dangerous for me to return here, but I can't leave my family again. And now that I know about you…"

He nods. "But as the village elder, and even as your father, if I can call myself that, the best option I see is for you to leave again tonight and return to Rabba. I'll write a letter for you to take, telling him the truth about you. You can carry on tanning or we could help you find another trade. I would visit you as often as I could, and I'm sure the same is true for your mother and Timaeus."

I nod. "That's wise advice," I say. "But I'm tired of running and I still haven't done what the Master told me to do. He said that I should tell my family and our village about the Master. I need to ask them for their forgiveness."

"Phin, even if they don't take you out and stone you, they'll inform the soldiers about you. You'll still be on the run."

He's right. Why am I being so stubborn? I'm just thinking about how to answer when Tehinah's wife steps in. She peers closer and then recognizes who I am and screams.

Tehinah tries to shush her, although they're sure to have a neighbour or two knock on their compound door any moment now, checking that everything's all right. "What's he doing here?" she hisses, backing away from me. Tehinah talks to her calmly, trying to explain that I'm no longer a threat, that the spirits have left me and I've returned to make amends. Then someone knocks at the door and calls out to see if everything is all right. Tehinah looks pleadingly at his wife, but she's already at the door letting them in.

Before I know it, I'm back in the cell next to their compound for my own protection, and I know that news of my return will spread through the village like wildfire.

"This is what I was afraid of," says Tehinah through the window bars, as he unlocks the padlock and lifts the bar on the door to bring me a steaming bowl of stew. He's posted the one foreign soldier in our village on guard outside, probably to keep him from running off and informing other soldiers. At least he never saw what I was like before, when the spirits lived in me. "I'll do my best to convince the village that you cannot be held responsible for your actions. We all heard the different voices speaking out of you and saw your strength. We all know that none of that was humanly possible. Phin, pray to your God tonight. The village will gather at first light tomorrow to listen to you."

After Tehinah leaves, I sit at an angle so I can see some stars through the window bars on the door. Then I pray. I remember the other times I was imprisoned in this cell. Now I feel so different. I'm at peace and I know that I'm finally doing what the Master told me to do. I pray for Tehinah and for my family and for some kind of resolution tomorrow.

At some point, I fall asleep. I'm jolted awake as something sharp smacks against my cheek. I put my hand to my face and wipe away the smear of rotten apricot. Its stone has made me bleed a little. Another rotten apricot hits one of the window bars and spatters everywhere. The cell is filled with a rotten, sweet smell. Then I notice the shouting. I can tell from the volume that most of the village must already be outside. I get up and decide to use the bucket latrine now, so that I'm ready for when they call me out. I've barely finished when I hear the key turn and the door open. It's Tehinah.

"I'm going to tie your hands," he says, raising his voice against the crowd outside. "Don't worry, I won't tie them tightly. It's just to reassure them."

I offer him my hands. "I don't know how reassuring this rope will be when I used to break out of metal chains," I say.

He smiles grimly. "I'll speak to the village first. I'm going to tell them that I take you as my ward and assume full responsibility for all your future actions."

A lump forms in my throat. "Thank you," I say.

"Not now," he replies brusquely. He can't afford displays of emotion right now. He ducks out, closing the door behind him, returning with several of the burliest men in the village. I recognize the blacksmith, who eyes me warily.

"Don't worry, I'm safe," I say. But it doesn't make any difference.

They gather around me and then Tehinah walks me out. Another rotten apricot catches me just above my left eye, spattering all over my face, bringing a cheer from the crowd. Tehinah's men push the crowd back while one of them helps Tehinah upturn a large wooden pallet to use as a platform. He climbs onto it and holds his hands up for silence.

Then he does exactly what he promised. He starts by asking the crowd if they are happy for him to remain their village elder and to conduct this impromptu town council. That soon has everyone cheering for him, and that's when he declares his intentions of taking me on as his ward, taking full personal responsibility for anything I might do. People mutter to each other, wondering why he would be willing to help this monster.

"I remember what those spirits inside him did to me," Tehinah shouts, and suddenly he doesn't look quite so old and weary any more. A hand strays to his broken nose. "And I've heard from Phin himself about what they did to him." He turns to me. "Take off your tunic," he says. He has to untie my hands. He points at the scar marks criss-crossing my chest. "If we could punish these spirits, we would, after all they've done to him and all they've done to us. But we cannot demand justice from spirits and nor is it right to punish the victims. Phineas is just another of these victims. You appointed me as your elder, and I'm asking you now to listen to what he has to say."

The crowd quietens. I realize that most of them actually want to hear from me. They may hate me, but they're also surprised and curious about why I've come back. I used to be a monster to them. They've seen me bring down a whole section of soldiers. So, now that I have their attention, I ask for the Master's gift to help me, and then I begin. "You must think I'm mad to come back here after everything that's happened," I say. "Or maybe you think the spirits have returned to me and that I don't need to fear you or anyone else. Neither of those things is true. I want to tell you why I've come back; what makes me risk my life to be here now. But I need to start with the night my mother's husband, Aqub, came home angry and drunk."

I pause, scanning the crowd. People of all ages are here. No one wants to miss this. Some of the youths still hold rotting, dripping fruit in their hands, no longer interested in these potential missiles when they can hear the monster tell his story. A couple of pig-herders still yell for justice, but others in the crowd shout back at them to be quiet. Who doesn't remember the last time I stood before them, naked and chained, and what I did next?

I see Mother with Verutia on her hip and Berenice clutching her swollen belly as they weave their way through the crowd, ignoring the looks of others, and jostling to come as close to me as they can. Towards the back of the crowd I can just make out Rufus and Timaeus and others in his crew. They've put down their baskets of fish and now Timaeus is also working his way through the crowd to get closer to me. They are willing to stand by me as I face the village, and I have to stop thinking about it otherwise my voice will crack with emotion and I won't be able to carry on.

I swallow, wipe a tear from my eye and begin. I've never spoken to so many people at once. I should be nervous. I'm not that great with words, but somehow the story flows. Again I don't tell everything, but when it comes to me killing Aqub, I take some responsibility. It may have been the spirits inside me, but I still really wanted him dead. I tell them what it was like each time people came for me, and how the spirits would fill me with unnatural strength. I tell them how awful it was to be trapped in my own body. Then I talk about the cutting and how I kept trying to kill myself.

"I did terrible things," I say. "Some of you who are standing right here experienced this. I did unforgiveable things to you. I wish I could take them back. I wish I hadn't been a prisoner to the spirits inside me." I hear a woman sob nearby, and a man beside her puts his arm around her as she weeps into his shoulder. I don't even know her name, but I recognize her as one of the women I once attacked and beat up in the field.

"I lost all hope, even the hope of death. I wasn't a person any more. I wasn't even an animal. I don't know what I was. All I know is that I was desperate for my life to be over. And yet, here I am today asking you to listen to me and maybe even give me a second chance to live here again. I want to try to make up for some of the hurt I've caused." I pause and the crowd is completely silent. "Now I want to tell you how I was freed from those spirits."

And so I explain about the night of the storm that suddenly ceased and how I could feel the spirits within me and their terror of the Master and his power. I tell of his great love and kindness to me. How he came through the storm to help me.

"Don't you know what your 'Master' has done to our village?" I hear a voice spit, full of venom and anger. It's a voice I recognize. It's Antigona. Her face is red with rage, and spittle flies with each word. "You have ruined and bankrupted us!"

"Let him finish, Antigona," Tehinah calls out, but already the crowd is stirred. I look around uneasily. I can feel the change in mood. I glance down at Mother and Berenice, who both look anxious, but then I'm distracted by Timaeus. He looks up at me, face drawn in concern, but then he glances above me and his eyes suddenly widen in terror. "No!" he screams and I'm about to turn around but then there's a thud and everything goes dark.

I don't understand what's happening. I thought I knew what darkness was but this is so utter and total. So is the silence. I can't even hear the pounding of my own heart or the sound of my breath. I try to look around me, to figure out what's happening, but I've lost all sense of my body.

Then suddenly there's a tunnel of sound and light and I'm rushing towards it. I'm jettisoned into chaos. At first, all I can see is tight, curly hair, slick with blood. I can hear screaming. I seem to be moving backwards and now my mother comes into view. She's wailing and holding me in her hands. Blood spreads around her and I worry for a moment that it'll stain the robe she's wearing.

Something's not right and it takes me a moment to realize that I'm seeing myself, but that this isn't possible. Berenice lifts my limp hand and puts it to her face, smearing blood against her cheek. She screams and then flings a handful of dust in the air over her head. I want to help them, to put my arms around them and comfort them, and to show them that I'm here, alive, but I keep moving further away.

Then I see Rufus and the other fishermen holding Timaeus back. His eyes and neck veins bulge as he roars, "No! No!" and tries to launch himself towards the platform where I was standing.

I hear Tehinah's voice as he comes into view. "Get him down from there," he sobs, and then I see Justus with two of his friends standing on the flat cell roof that was behind me. The other two youths still hold large, sharp rocks in their hands, but Justus's hands are empty. He has a grim smile on his face as he looks down, and doesn't even notice Tehinah's men placing a ladder against the roof or the rotten apricot that hits his robe and stains it dark yellow.

"Give them space," shouts one person.

"Let me through," shouts Tehinah, coming to my side and taking my limp hand from Berenice, feeling frantically for a pulse. "No," he whispers, still desperately searching for it. "No!" he screams, and that really makes the crowd step back. Little Verutia just stands beside Berenice wailing, terrified and forgotten.

I try to run to them, to my family. To my new father. I want to let them know that I'm here, but I can't. *No!* I try to shout, but I have no voice. I seem to be floating away. I try kicking as if I was diving in water and wanting to swim down to the bottom of the lake. Nothing happens – I just keep gaining height. Then I see what looks like a flock of birds or bats or perhaps living rags, swooping and diving over the heads of the crowd, screeching and crowing. One of them passes me, cackling, "What a feast, what a feast!"

No! I try to scream, but still there's no sound. I'm panicking now. I just want to get back to my family. That can't really be me down there. I need to wake up and show them I'm all right. I need to let them nurse me back to health. Then we'll have today and tomorrow and the day after that, and we'll keep living and I'll be with them and we'll learn how to be a family together again, and I'll know what it feels like to have a father, and slowly the village will forgive and accept me. That's what's supposed to happen. Not this.

Some of the spirits begin to notice me, although most are drunk and crazed on the pain and chaos of the crowd below. One of the larger spirits flies towards me. "What have you done?" it snarls. "Look what you've unleashed." Its face is full of rage as it dives away from me. Then I notice how many of the crowd have gathered around Mother, kneeling with her and throwing dust over their heads, ululating in grief. There are more than I would have expected, including that woman who cried earlier when she saw me. Maybe the Master is using my words already, sowing seeds that will grow. I think of Malchus and how his family now follow The Way. This just makes me even more determined to get back there so I can help these seeds to grow.

Instead, I'm gaining height. *Please, let me go back!* I shout silently. It's a prayer of sorts. How can I abandon my family now, just when we're about to start again? Then I hear a voice above me calling my name. I turn my gaze. I'm able to do that. At first I just see the blaze of the rising sun, but then I look closer. Shimmering in the blaze is the Master. I hear him calling me, his arms outstretched, welcoming me.

My heart soars, but still I look back at the crowd below. "Please, let me go back to them," I cry out. I find I can speak now. I remember that moment on the lake shore when I stared at the embers of his fire, his footprints in the sand and the diminishing silhouette of his boat, and how much I longed to be with him. The last place I wanted to return to was my village, but now I'm so desperate to get back to living. "They need me. Someone has to tell them about you."

"I will not forget them," the Master says. I look at him again and see that his outstretched arms have horrible scars on them from where he was nailed. Even though he glows and is almost too bright for me to look at, he's still the same man I once met. I glance down at my wrists. They seem solid again, and the golden bonds the Master placed on them in my vision glow brightly. "Can you trust me with your family?"

I glance back. The crowd look like ants gathered around a discarded crumb.

"I love them no less than I love you," he says. And I know it's true. I feel a sudden sense of peace as I move towards him.

"Come," he says. His arms are open wide, and his voice is rich with love. I feel joy welling up in me, and my heart soars. He is eclipsing my pain and regret with his presence. The tiny people below me and the huge expanse of water seem to dim. Like an athlete who has almost reached the finishing line, I begin to run. I don't know how I run on air, but I feel myself getting closer. "Come," he calls, and I realize that no chain or manacle can ever hold me back again. This is my time. He is my prize.

Manacle

"I'm coming, Master," I shout. "I'm coming!" If I had a flat basket and turban in my hands they'd be streaming behind me like a banner.

I run to him unfettered, and I've never felt more alive.

In loving memory of Endre Medhaug –
a race I wish had lasted longer.

Acknowledgments

This story is based on accounts found in the Gospel of Mark (chapter 5) and the Gospel of Luke (chapter 8). You can access them for free at www.biblegateway.com. I was inspired by *The Victor* by Patricia St John (Scripture Union, 1983), which I read as a child and it has stayed with me. Her novel showed me the powerful narrative interplay between darkness and light.

Like Phin, I've roamed around a fair bit in the writing of this story, fitting it around studies and student holidays. I started writing in Oxford and then continued in Cambridge, before moving further afield to Osh in Kyrgyzstan and then Khiva in Uzbekistan. Thanks in particular to Steve and Becca Scott and their wonderful family for letting me write in their home in Osh, helping me strike a balance between beavering away at this story in their spare room, and then coming out for air, people and food, and to my lovely Uzbek family. I'm also grateful to my parents for letting me set up camp at their dining room table once more.

Historical fiction allows for speculation, but in no way is this story supposed to be a definitive guide to the spirit world. I wrote it because I was so surprised that Jesus listens to the unclean spirits and does what they ask, then listens to the Gentile village people who ask him to leave, and obliges. Then, when the unnamed demoniac so horribly afflicted begs Jesus to take him with him, Jesus says no. Why? It seems so unfeeling. Instead he sends him back to his family and community. I wanted to explore what came next and also what had happened before. Can we come back from the wrongs of the past?

I probably owe an apology to those who felt Phin deserved a happy ending after everything he went through. I wept when

I realized that my original conclusion wouldn't cut it. However, Phin running to the Master really is the ultimate "happily ever after" if you think about it. I felt that I had to be true to the stories of unheralded and yet incredibly courageous followers of the teacher around the world who suffer and are often killed for their faith. Lives of ease are the exception, not the norm.

Gratitude to Richard Bauckham for his inventory of first-century Palestinian names, as found in *Jesus and the Eyewitnesses* (Eerdmans, 2008), which I have once again pillaged.

Thanks again to my editor, Jessica Tinker, copy editor, Sheila Jacobs, and illustrator, Sarah J. Coleman. Also special thanks to Anne de la Hunty, Erin Crider, Rev. Sue Hope, Sue Donnelly, Helen Jackson, Tiffany Graves, Emma Goode, Emma Lowth and Jane Spiro for your helpful insights, suggestions and mistake-spotting. You've definitely improved this novel. A third instalment is on its way. I still haven't figured out a decent title for it, though.